W9-BXX-019

The
Autum
VOLUME
ONE

nlands
Tooth and Claw

By

Kurt Busiek
Writer

and

Benjamin Dewey
Artist

Jordie Bellaire
Colors

John Roshell of Comicraft
Design & Lettering

image

Kaark.

God-
killer.

Kaark.

B. DEWEY © 2014

FOR BENJAMIN DEWEY:
LINDSEY ELLIS
Production Assistant

FOR JORDIE BELLAIRE:
JEONG JOO PARK &
CHAN SOO *of* YESFLAT
Flatters

FOR COMICRAFT:
JIMMY BETANCOURT &
ALBERT DESCHESNE
Lettering

KYLER TANOWITZ
Production Assistant

RICHARD STARKINGS
President & First Tiger

THE AUTUMNLANDS Volume One: TOOTH & CLAW. First Printing, July 2015. Published by Image Comics, Inc. Office of publication: 2001 Center Street, Sixth Floor, Berkeley, CA 94704. Printed in the USA. For information regarding the CPSIA on this printed material call: 203-595-3636 and provide reference # RICH-622320
For international rights contact foreignlicensing@imagecomics.com

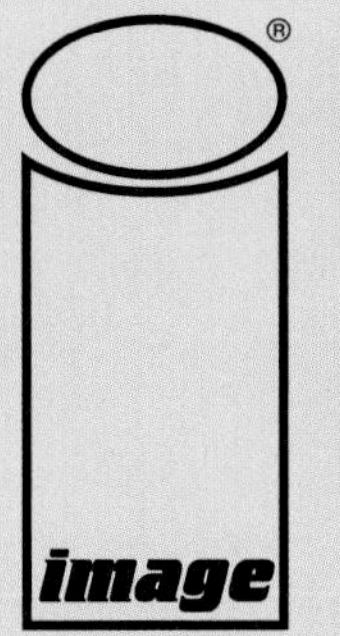

One

HERE'S WHAT YOU NEED TO *KNOW* ABOUT US –

WE WERE *GOOD* AND *GENTLE CREATURES.*
LOVING AND *FEARING* OUR GODS, DUTIFUL AND *OBEDIENT.*

CLINK

LIVING UP TO THEIR *LAWS* AND *EDICTS* THE BEST WE COULD.

AND THE *WIZARDS*, THAT DAY –

– THEY WERE TRYING TO SAVE THE WORLD. TO *RESTORE* IT TO WHAT IT ONCE WAS.

THEY TRULY *WERE* –

In the
Sevente

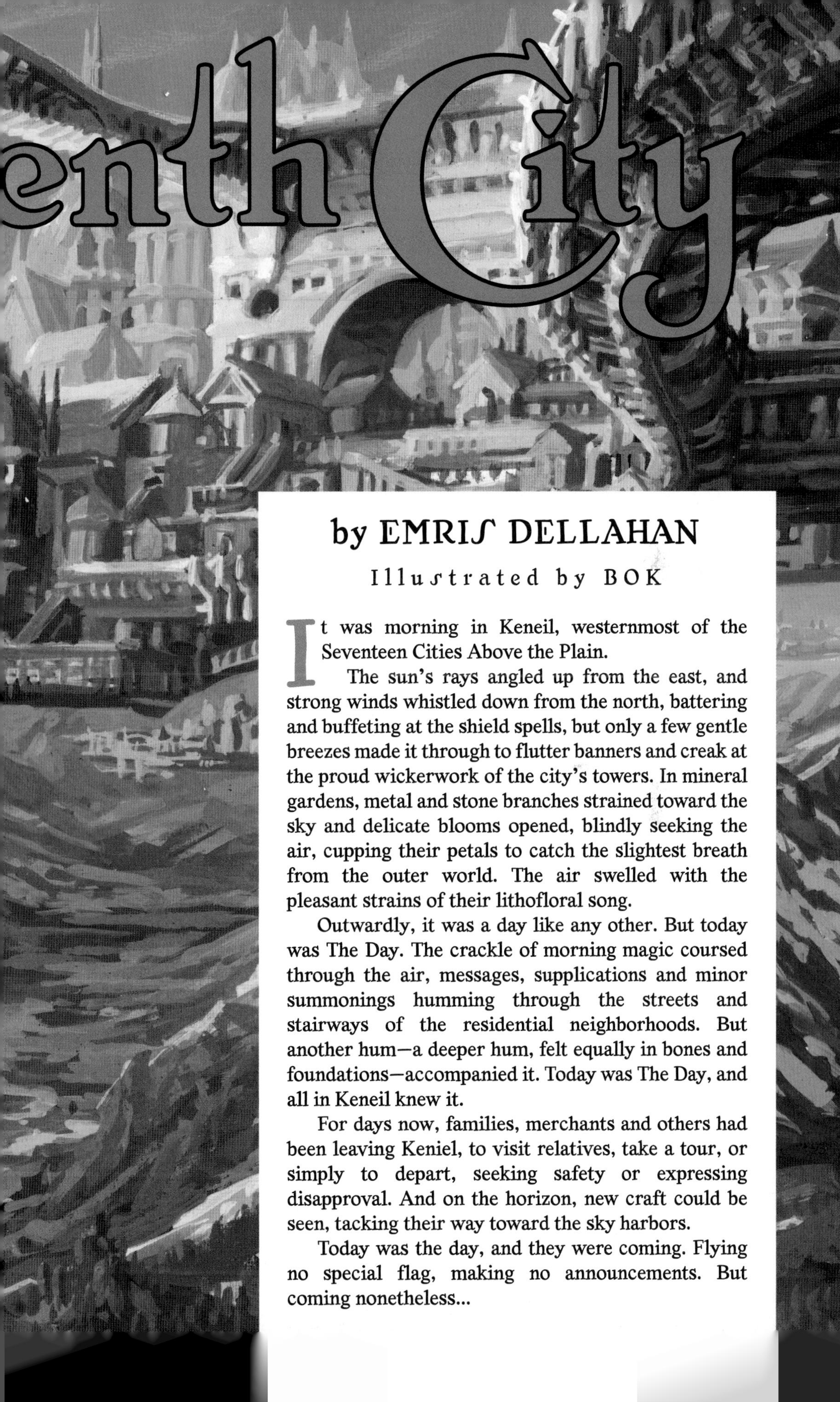

by EMRIS DELLAHAN

Illustrated by BOK

It was morning in Keneil, westernmost of the Seventeen Cities Above the Plain.

The sun's rays angled up from the east, and strong winds whistled down from the north, battering and buffeting at the shield spells, but only a few gentle breezes made it through to flutter banners and creak at the proud wickerwork of the city's towers. In mineral gardens, metal and stone branches strained toward the sky and delicate blooms opened, blindly seeking the air, cupping their petals to catch the slightest breath from the outer world. The air swelled with the pleasant strains of their lithofloral song.

Outwardly, it was a day like any other. But today was The Day. The crackle of morning magic coursed through the air, messages, supplications and minor summonings humming through the streets and stairways of the residential neighborhoods. But another hum—a deeper hum, felt equally in bones and foundations—accompanied it. Today was The Day, and all in Keneil knew it.

For days now, families, merchants and others had been leaving Keniel, to visit relatives, take a tour, or simply to depart, seeking safety or expressing disapproval. And on the horizon, new craft could be seen, tacking their way toward the sky harbors.

Today was the day, and they were coming. Flying no special flag, making no announcements. But coming nonetheless...

THAT MORNING, I DID THE THIRTY-TWO-AND-ONE DAILY OBEISANCES FOR MY FAMILY, AS WAS MY DUTY.

SWEET FRUIT FOR DILIDI-I, GODDESS OF HEALTH, EDUCATION AND WELFARE, WHO WATCHES OVER OUR BODIES, OUR MINDS.
AND TO IDENTE, THE ONE ABOVE ALL.

THE SMOKE OF INDUSTRY FOR THE *SISTERS,* THE TWO-HEADED GODDESS OF *HOUSING,* AND OF *URBAN DEVELOPMENT.*

AND FOR *IDENTE,* THE ONE ABOVE ALL.

PRAYERS TO *TOFAR,* ROUGH-HEWN UNDERGOD OF *WILDLIFE AND FISHERIES.* DANCE FOR *PETOSH,* GOD OF *COMMERCE.*

AND ALL THE OTHERS, AND IDENTE AS WELL.
I'D GROWN SWIFT AT IT, WITHOUT UNSEEMLY HASTE, IN MY YEAR OF BEING HONORED WITH THE DUTY.
LASTLY THE CHANT TO ARDUNN, GOD OF HOMELAND SECURITY, FOR OUR CONTINUED SAFETY AND STRENGTH. AND TO –
DUNSTAN! DON'T DRAG YOUR TAIL, LAD! WE'LL BE LATE!

Y-yes, father!
I HAD NEVER BEFORE BEEN PERMITTED TO *ACCOMPANY* HIM ON SUCH AN IMPORTANT DAY –

Punctuality is important, Dunstan. Imperfection in behavior is a sign of weakness.
Yes, father.

When dealing with the *lesser ones*, you must show no frailty, no error.
If you are to oversee trade one day, too, you must learn this.
Trade-master.
Trade-master.

DOWNWARD WE WENT, AND –

We are here.
Um – uh –
Calm, Dunstan. Controlled. Always.

Ho.
Ho, cloud-dweller.
We labor long to fill your needs. Three time normal quantities, and little warning. But all here. All ready, as you ask.

You have done well, Seven-Scars.
We of the Cities Above shall speak your name kindly to the gods.
Tuk.

Your payment.
I thank, dweller in –

Hrn? This – not *enough!*

It is the promised amount. Enough magic for your healers, and for your warders to guard your –
Not *enough!* We work, sweat – thin herds! Three *time* what normally delivered! *Three!* And this – this –

It is the promised amount.

Uh –

Show no fear, Dunstan. It will ruin you for future dealings with them.
But –

We will not deal with Seven-Scars again. Choose *another* among you to speak with us henceforth.
Come, Dunstan...

...we're done here.

I knew something like this would happen.
This is why you came along, to see more of what the job requires.
The lesser ones serve us, my son, as we serve the gods. They are not to be allowed to forget this. Ever.

But — if it really is three times what we usually —
We're not made of magic, Dunstan. They seek to husband their takings, until they can rebel against us. This, we can never allow.
You understand?
Uh — I think so —
Good. Then go watch the arrivals. I know you've been panting to.

Heh. Pups.

Look, **LOOK!**
There! No, there — from *Santara*, I'd bet on it —

Did I miss any, Kev? Did I miss them?
Only a few. But look at 'em — they're crowding in —

THEY CAME FROM ALL THE OTHER CITIES. NO ONE WAS FLYING THEIR COLORS. THEY DIDN'T WANT THEIR *PRESENCE* KNOWN.
SOME LOOKED *FIERCE,* AS IF CHALLENGING ANYONE TO STOP THEM —
— AND SOME LIKE THEY WERE SCARED SOMEONE *WOULD.*
BUT WE ALL *KNEW* WHY THEY WERE THERE.

ANYONE WITH WIZARD PARENTS, OR UNCLES, OR ANYTHING — ANYONE WHO'D OVERHEARD *KNEW.* IT WAS ONLY WEEKS AGO, AT THE *GRAND COLLOQUY...*

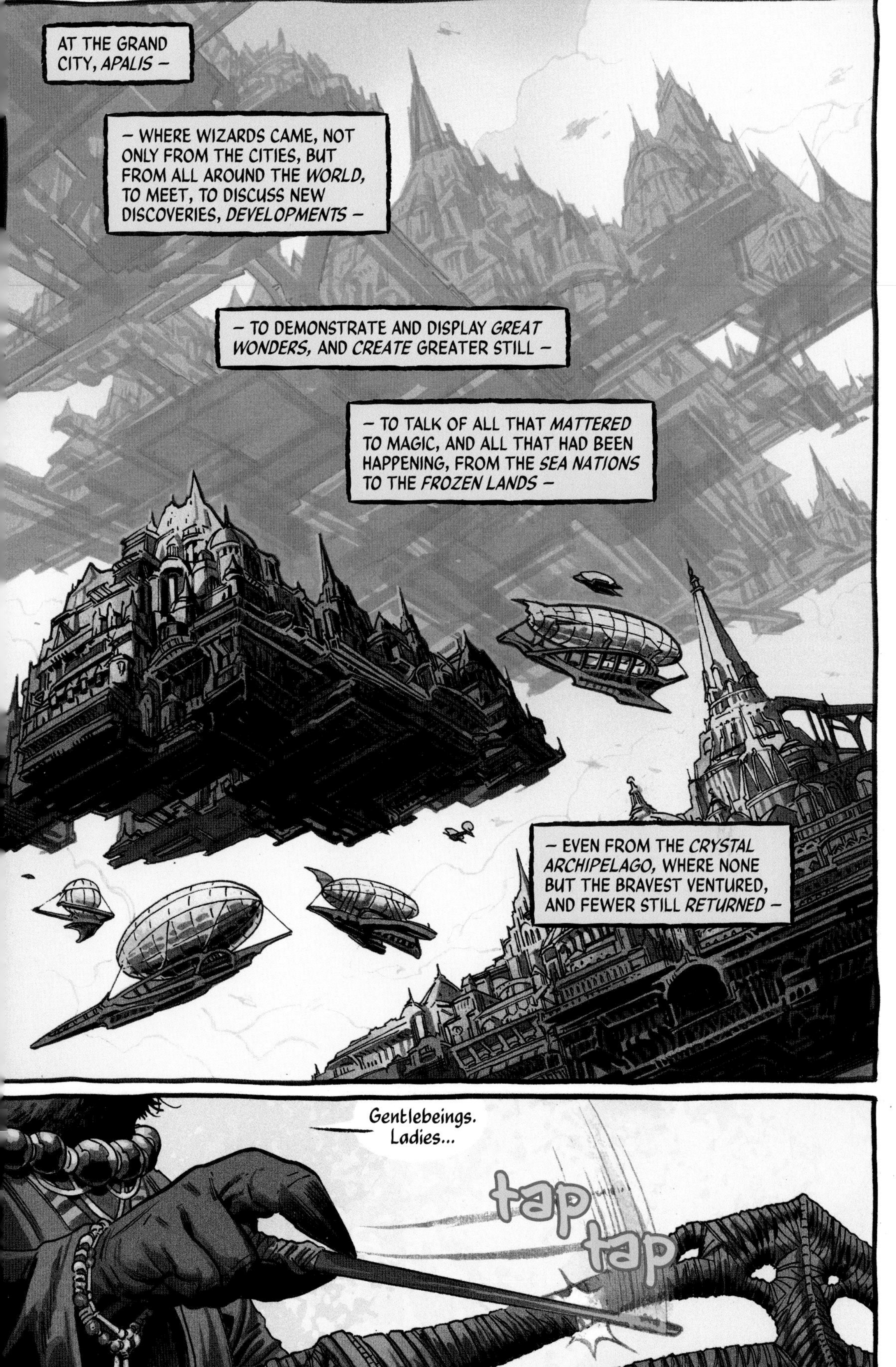
AT THE GRAND CITY, APALIS –
– WHERE WIZARDS CAME, NOT ONLY FROM THE CITIES, BUT FROM ALL AROUND THE WORLD, TO MEET, TO DISCUSS NEW DISCOVERIES, DEVELOPMENTS –
– TO DEMONSTRATE AND DISPLAY GREAT WONDERS, AND CREATE GREATER STILL –
– TO TALK OF ALL THAT MATTERED TO MAGIC, AND ALL THAT HAD BEEN HAPPENING, FROM THE SEA NATIONS TO THE FROZEN LANDS –
– EVEN FROM THE CRYSTAL ARCHIPELAGO, WHERE NONE BUT THE BRAVEST VENTURED, AND FEWER STILL RETURNED –
Gentlebeings. Ladies...
tap
tap

I apologize for interrupting this delightful luncheon.
But the Colloquy was unable to find room in the schedule for me to speak, so I must make some time.
I am *Gharta of Daiir*, known as The Seeker. You all know me, or know of me. I am...not of a retiring nature.

It is fading, it has been fading for centuries, and unless something is done, many among us may live to see the end of it.
And with its passing, so comes the end of our way of life.

Are you ready, my august fellow practitioners?
For our spells to fail? For the famines that will follow?
For upheaval and war and starvation? To be reduced from seekers of wisdom and truth to withered, diseased –

And what shall we do? What shall we do?!
A thousand thousand spells have been tried. And have failed!
Shall we starve ourselves?
Live on a bare trickle of magic, in hopes of extending it further?

Hneh. A little starvation wouldn't hurt you any, Pelobos of the North Coast.
HA HA HA
But no. I speak not to counsel despair – nor to offer defeatist plans to eke ever more utility from our dwindling power.

Attend...

The **GREAT CHAMPION,** gentlebeings.
Our history, our legends...they all speak of him. The hero who, facing the world's destruction and certain death, opened the gates of magic, and brought its power to us.
The champion who did what we need to do *again.* But we do not know how.

My lady- and gentle-wizards of the Seventeen Cities, we are going to repair all.
We are going to *bring back* the Great Champion. And have him open those gates *once more.*
Madness –
Sheer *madness* –
It can't be *done* –
Magic *can't* reach back to before it existed –
Not possible –
Tried *before,* time and again –
Sheer folly of a *damaged* –
But it can be done.
IT CAN BE DONE.
Not by one wizard working alone, no. But a team, working together – combining spells, enhancing them –
You know my work with combinatory magics. I've devised a scheme – it will take at least sixteen wizards, working in concert.
We will introduce Tentacular Drift through the –
No.

First-in-Council Tallon!
If the gods meant us to reach back to before the time of magic, Gharta the Seeker –
– then surely it would have happened by now.

They would have allowed it long since. Nay, they would have guided our hands. But they have not.
To essay this is blasphemy. It is forbidden.
Tallon, the gods have not spoken for 257 years. They cannot have forbidden any such –

You will address me as 'First-in-Council,' Gharta. Or 'High One.' And your 'scheme' is rejected.
Don't be absurd, Tallon. You can't block a legitimate sorcerous inquiry into –

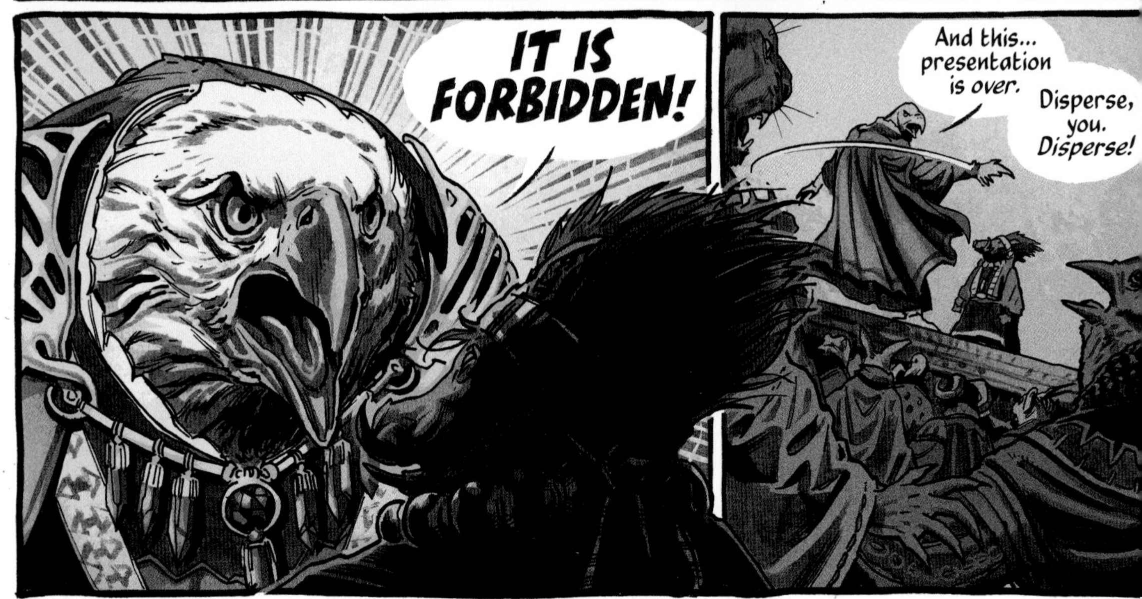
IT IS FORBIDDEN!
And this... presentation is *over.*
Disperse, you. *Disperse!*

FIRST-IN-COUNCIL TALLON'S WORD WAS AS *LAW*, AND NONE DARED CHALLENGE IT *OPENLY*.
BUT GHARTA OF DHAIIR'S INTERRUPTED PRESENTATION WAS THE *TALK* OF THE COLLOQUY, TAFFY'S FATHER TOLD HER –
– AND ONE BY ONE, OR IN GROUPS, WIZARD AFTER WIZARD FOUND REASON TO *TALK* WITH GHARTA.
IF SHE COULD DO WHAT SHE SAID SHE COULD, IT WOULD MAKE *HISTORY*. IT WOULD BE THE GREATEST SORCEROUS FEAT SINCE THE *DAWN OF MAGIC*.
AND A CHANCE TO BE A *PART* OF IT –

Yes, yes. A small, tightly-knit group. With the right skills...
Can you believe this? What is she, a jumped-up little warthog from the savannahs somewhere?
And *she's* going to save the world?

Hneh. Clearly, she can't even master the elegance spells to make herself look like a *real* wizard...

Hmph. Quite right, quite right. And it's not really *that* much of a breakthrough, of course.
I played around with combinatory patterns a bit at school. Wasn't as impressed with them as she is.

I daresay I could teach her a thing or two...
Hneh. But Sands, why would you want to?

And it's appalling. She's talking to just *anyone.*
Rude, really, making us wait.

Serve her right if we just up and left...

THUS IT BEGAN –

– AND HERE THEY ALL CAME, TO THE MOST REMOTE OF THE *SEVENTEEN CITIES,* THE FARTHEST FROM THE COUNCIL SEAT –

Welcome, welcome.
Come in, and see...

This will be our staging area.
That's — the Pattern of Leng!
Yes. Never before constructed at this size. Took several tries to make it hold together.
But — it's so —
But we'll need it to create a melding environment, where we can combine and harmonize all the main spells.

The main focus will be Tulla's Spell of Vulvular Dilation...
...but it must be sublimated to the Archway of Centuries.
Yes, that will be difficult. Quite difficult.

But it is only the start.
We must then maintain contact with the era of magic, allowing tendrils of it to reach through into the past...
...using VanDahl's Tentacular Drift.

Resistance, you say? What can there be to resist the Drift, in an age before magic?
That part should be easy.
Of course, we will not be able to touch the Champion — or anything else solid — directly, of course. No magic to adhere to.

But once we've drifted enough magic into the air around him, I'll solidify it with the Spell of the Unremitting Pearl...
...and, well, the rest should be self-explanatory.

Ludvic, Adaal, you'll perform the Dilation, with Ramaat framing the Archway. You four, I'll need on the Drift.
We'll run through it this afternoon, including when to incarnate the Gauntlets of Faria...
And my role...?

Ah, yes, we talked before. You are...
Sandorst of Samia! Sandorst the *Exacting?* Third Councillor of Telm?
I did not expect to be left waiting, while other, lesser talents were –

Of course, of course. Sandorst.
The procedure will generate stifling, potentially killing heat.

We need a team generating Pak's Wintry Winds, to –
I am to be doing menial support work? I, Sandorst?
Eh? I'd understood you were a premier atmospherics talent. But if you're unwilling, there are others who might –

NO!
Hrmph. No, if history is to be made, it will require our *finest* talents. I consent to lead this team.

Enna! Bring the bags – we go to the inn!
Yes, father.

Come along, we don't have all day! Now where is that god-rotted inn?
Here, let me help.
Inn of the Three Chimes, I bet? I'll show you the way.
Th-thank you –!

No problem.
And later, I can show you the best place to watch it all from!

To watch...?

YES, WE WATCHED –
It's right around here...

...see? There are gaps in the hedge. Wickerwalls, here and there.
Quick, Dusty! They just finished an invocation to the eidolons of Ways and Means, asking their favor!
They're starting!

Oh...
...oh!
Very good, Ramaat. Feel the Pattern as you build the Archway. Let the Vulvular Dilation be a part of your spell –
– let it anchor to the edges of the Arch –

A bit more intensity, Ludvic. Match Adaal's rhythm — tease the dilation open slowly, evenly.
Begin the winds, Sandorst. A breeze at first...
AND THERE IT WAS. A SIGHT UNSEEN FOR MILLENNIA. THAT NO ONE THOUGHT IT WAS EVEN POSSIBLE TO SEE.
AN ACTUAL GLIMPSE OF THE GREAT CHAMPION —
I am beginning VanDahl's Tentacular Drift .
Maintain, gentlebeings, maintain. When the Drift hits the non-magical region, there will be a drain on the Pattern.
There will be heat. Compensate, and...
AAH!
The Pattern! It writhes! It —
Maintain! Feed it, Allatar! Strengthen it, calm it —
Keep it smooth, keep it open —
I COULDN'T BELIEVE IT —
THERE'D BEEN SO MUCH DEBATE THROUGHOUT HISTORY. WHAT BREED OF BEAST WAS THE CHAMPION? AND NOW WE'D KNOW.

Hnn...
T-too hot –
SANDORST! THE WINDS!
I WAS TAUGHT HIS LOYALTY, HIS *TENACITY*, MARKED HIM AS FROM THE DOG TRIBES. BUT *EVERY* TRIBE CLAIMED HIM. THERE HAD BEEN *WARS* OVER IT.
THE EAGLES, THE BEARS. EVEN THE *IGUANA* TRIBES. AND NOW –

It –
It's truly –

SANDORST! BY ALL THE GODS, SANDORST! THE WINDS!
he's –
I can't – c-can't hold –

DO IT! HOLD IT!
THE PATTERN, THE ARCHWAY! DO NOT FLINCH!

Uh!
Th-the winds, you fools! The winds!
Now, you sluggards!

Ahh!
hlkk

I HAVE HIM! THE GAUNTLETS, TELLA! NOW!
I NEED ONLY SECONDS - SECONDS TO FORM THE UNREMITTING PEARL, AND PULL -

I – I have –

Wh-what — ?
Th-the Pattern! It —

K-KRMMBB...

What – what just –
The Pattern – needed more power than they could *feed* to it. So it reached out –

It *drained* – it drained the city-spells –
Gharta! What have you done, sow?! We're –

Gharta! The levitation spells have failed! You have to –
I can't! I have it – I have the Pearl! The rest of you –
The Pattern – fraying –
Dunstan –
Got you –
The shield-spells, at least!
Help me strengthen them, before –
Yes! Yes! Draw the leftover magic and feed it to –

IT SEEMED – IT SEEMED
SO *SILENT*, FOR SO LONG –

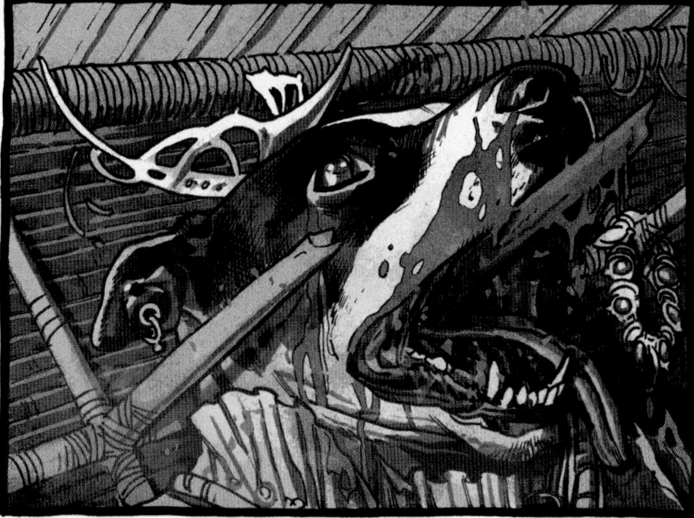

AND THEN – THERE WAS *BIRDSONG,* AND –

Wh –

Enn-enna? Kev?
Dusty?

WE SOUGHT – TO FIND FAMILY, OR FRIENDS –
BELLUS? Bellus, answer–!
Tana?

AND SOME WERE LUCKY.
Celia! CELIA!
Oh, Aska –

BUT SOME –

No...

no...

AFTER A WHILE, THEY STARTED FORMING *WORK PARTIES.*
I COULDN'T *JOIN* THEM. BUT THEY WERE BADLY NEEDED.

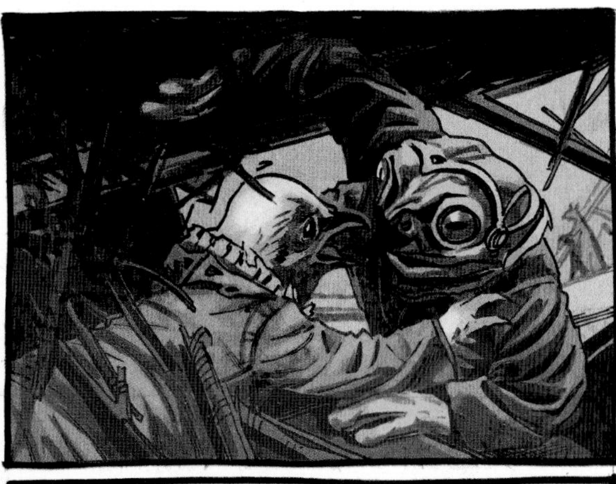

TO FREE *SURVIVORS.*

FIND *SUPPLIES.*

AND *FINALLY* –

– TO BURY OUR DEAD.
AND TO MOURN.

Under the ground.
The last place he would have wanted to be was under the ground...

He was going to take me to the Gulf Principates next month.
It would have been a buying trip. He was going to take me for the first time, show me my future duties.

We were going to travel. The Principates, the Galap Archipelago, the Horns. Even the Frozen Lands, maybe next year.
I was — he was going to — we were going to travel —
Dunstan...

This is Gharta's fault.
She tried the impossible. Failed to build in safeguards.
But *she* won't be blamed, oh no. She's safely *dead*, and —

Eh—?
BRMBLL

Hnuh.
Come here, everyone. Take a look...

The Unremitting Pearl.
We have it. We have him.

The cost was unimaginable.
But the salvation of the world is at hand.
Truly?
Within the Pearl – it is truly – ?

There is something within.
It is...male...and living...but like nothing I have sensed before...

He is within! It is he!
THE GREAT CHAMPION!

A tragic, momentous day.
I wish — I wish it had gone as planned. That the wizards fueling the archway had not buckled. That I foresaw our needs better.
But history is made.
And the world forever changed.

SHE WAS RIGHT.
THE WORLD *WAS* FOREVER CHANGED.

BUT THAT NIGHT, IN THE GLOW OF THAT *STRANGE, COMPELLING* LIGHT...

...WE HAD NO IDEA *HOW MUCH* IT WOULD CHANGE.

AND NO IDEA *AT ALL*...

Huh.
What's *that* all about, hm?
...WHERE IT WOULD ALL *LEAD* US.

TWO

"THE WALLS OF DiBANCA HAD BEEN *BREACHED.* THE SKIES *BLAZED* WITH MACHINE-FIRE. AND BELOW –

"– THE FOUL *RAMFASTI* WAITED, THEIR SHEENERIES AT THE READY. THIS WAS THE *END,* EVEN SUCH AS THEY KNEW.
"BUT THEY WOULD GO DOWN *FIGHTING.*

HOLD HIM BACK! HOLD HIM BACK! *He must not enter!*
"...SHOUTED THE WIZARD *NILOTICUS,* KNOWING A JOLT OF FEAR.
"THEY FOUGHT TO PROTECT THE *HEART.* THE PRIZE THEY HAD STOLEN. THE PRIZE THEY NEEDED TO *ENSLAVE THE WORLD.*

"BUT IN A CLATTER LIKE *THUNDER* AND A *MIGHTY LEAP,* HE WAS THERE –
Aah!
Aah!

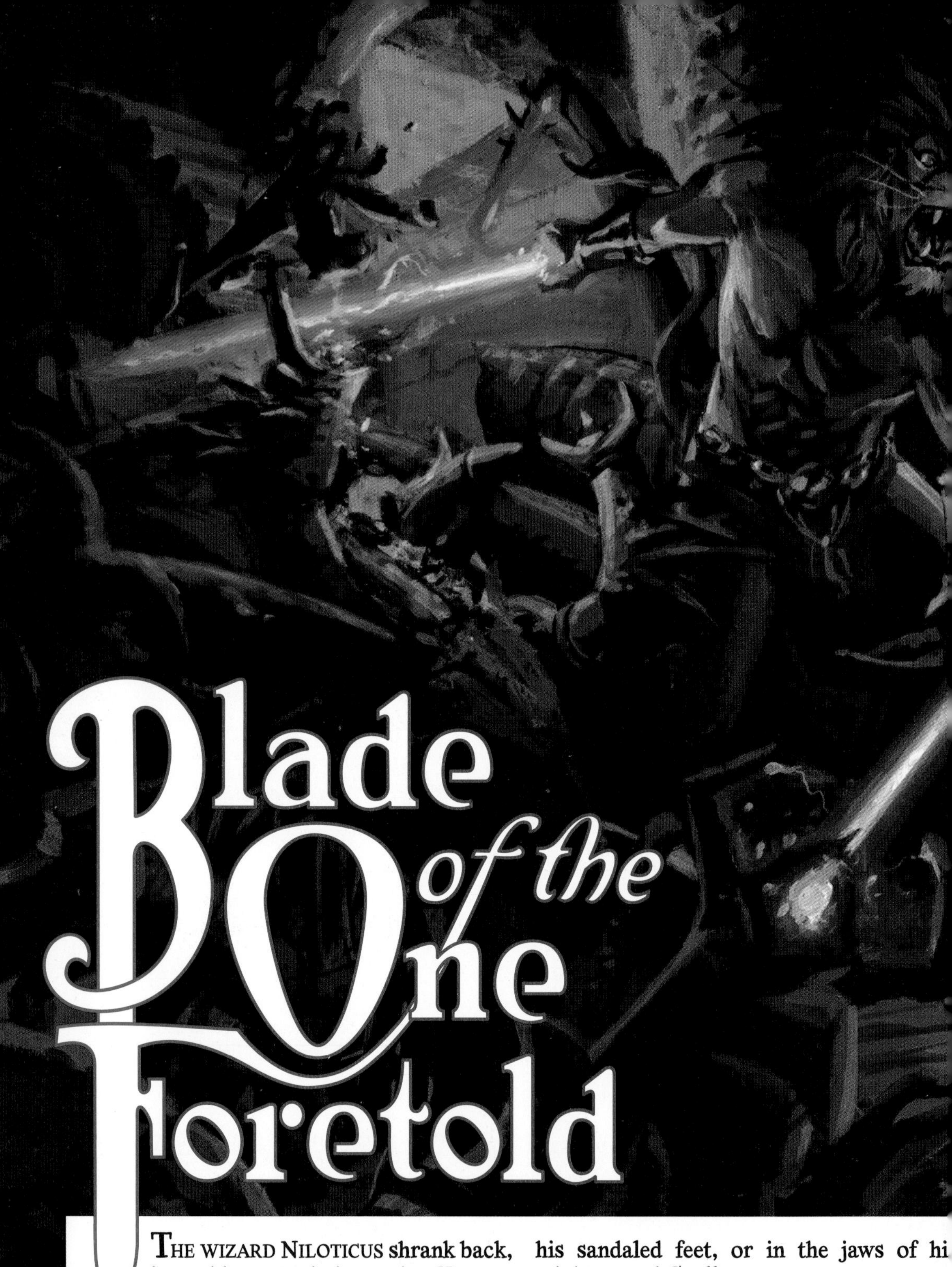

Blade of the One Foretold

THE WIZARD NILOTICUS shrank back, in sudden, atavistic panic. He was here. *He was here!*

The Great Champion laid about him with the Blade of Storms, and the foul Ramfasti fell before his relentless onslaught. They were the best their makers could offer, the pinnacle of enginery in a world that teemed with it. And still they fell, crushed beneath his sandaled feet, or in the jaws of hi mighty steed Grylla.

The Great Champion was there, and h would not be denied. The end of the lon battle was finally at hand.

•

He had sought the Heart of Az-Terassa across wondrous lands. Through burnin deserts of shimmering fire, through th

by MONAR T. WIRTHAS

Ursine Forests which none had lived to traverse, through ice-capped mountains where lurked ice-fanged jaws. They had thought it a new kind of enginery, a machinery that dwarfed all machineries that had come before, and they thought to dominate with it, to bring all before them to their knees.

But the Champion knew differently. He knew magic when he felt its call. And he knew it must be freed. To save Earth's peoples, to rebuild its shattered lands. To unleash wonders that could belong to no one ruler. He knew the Heart's true worth, and he was sworn to liberate it.

Niloticus snarled a deathspell, but the Champion vaulted over it. His blade swung back in one mighty arm...

Illustrated by GROZ GRAZZINI

...and even as the dead wizard's blood glistened on his feathers, the Champion strode forward, to the cage that held the Heart...
Feathers? His *mane,* you mean.

Everyone knows the Champion was of the lion tribes.
Lion tribes? Sure, one of the lion tribes that was all *forest diggers!*
A *blind digger?* Ha! That's such a —

Hsst.
No need to fight about it.

Maybe he *was* an eagle, like Enna's scholars say. Or a *greatwolf,* like in the Keneil Tapestry.
Or a lion, or bear.
Or a *mole!*

Right. Maybe even a mole. We don't know. *No one* knows. But if that wizardess Gharta and the others are right...
...we may be about to find out.

LITTLE WAS KNOWN OF THE *GREAT CHAMPION.*

ONLY THAT HE FOUGHT A *GREAT BATTLE,* AND LOOSED *MAGIC* INTO THE WORLD. AND THAT HE *DISAPPEARED,* LEAVING NO RECORD BEHIND.

BUT NOW, WE COULD ONLY *WONDER.* DID HE DISAPPEAR THROUGH *TIME?* WAS IT *WE* WHO CAUSED HIM TO –

Look! It – it –
CRIK-CRIKAKK

Nothing.
It fades...

This is your fault, wizardess. You destroyed a city, killed hundreds — and for what?
A corpse? Some insignificant hanger-on? The gods forbade this, Gharta, and you still —
Sandorst, really. This is not the time to —

Is it not truly him? Pecanna's reading said —
I can't see —
We must delve deeper through the Unremitting Pearl's shell. The Third Instance of Concentrated Sight should —

The Scrolls of Perceptos! I require them!
Someone bring —

Gentlebeings, gentlebeings.
Calm yourselves.

I am as eager as all of you to free our prize — and it is the Champion, I'm certain of it.
But we are alone in the Grand Foothills, at night, with no shelter but ruins. We have more immediate concerns.

Our first concern must be security. A message to the other cities, requesting rescue.
Pfeh.
Our energies are depleted from softening the crash! A message spell — how can we —

Pool our power, of course. Message spells burn hot, but we can manage that much.
Anyone with a little to spare, with me. *Now.*

AND —
...combined signet on the folds in *sevenlight*, a Remmearg twist, and...
...ah.

You've done it *right*? You're *certain*?
Bellamo's Third Supplication? I should *think* so. It was my first specialty.
The beacon is formed correctly. It describes our plight, our location and requests aid.

I'll just add *Delemm's Blessing*, to protect it in the event of any unexpected —

Cloud Dwellers brought low.
Cast down by own gods.

THIN NUMBERS! CULL HERD!
No, no!
Drive them back – drive them away!

HRAHAHH!

– WHOSE WILL WAS *THIS?*

Hra!
Dalvarr's Imprisoning Crystal! I can –
No! It draws too much power! You'll only weaken everyone else's –

KLDD

This way, Dunstan! We've got to get within the walls!
They — they hate us.
My father — he said we dealt with them fairly, treating them as they deserved, but —

Not now! Behind here!
But they — they —

— they hate us —
IT WAS BRUTAL — HORRIBLE —

Hn?

What in Zonomm's name — ?

CRIK-CRIKAKK
KRAKOWWK
Oh!
Oh...

HRRAAAAAAAAA
Urh?
What is?

Hlkk — !

Auhh?

gkk

Hell of the Thousand, what — ?

HE WAS –
HE WAS –
THERE WAS *SO MUCH BLOOD*, BUT HE DIDN'T EVEN SEEM TO *NOTICE* IT.

Urh?
NNRRRR...
Hruh?

NRH!
...RAAAAAH!

Aihhh!
SNAPT

HN-AIHHH!
HNH!

He's —
he's —

The great
Cham —

Tch-ahh!

nk

What? What is he sayi—
Telthan's Second Understanding! Quickly!
I have it!
— move! Fall the fuck back!
Uphill, behind the goddamn walls! Make it harder for them to reach you!
Don't attack, just defend! *Defend!* Leave them to *me!*
Leave them to — ?
K-aah!

Yes, yes!
Leave them to him!

BWAWWP

Come on, then.
Come on.

They weren't — weren't expecting any —
— any serious —

Nnn.

THERE HAD BEEN SO MUCH DEATH ALREADY. TOO MUCH TO THINK ABOUT.
AND NOW – NOW THERE WAS –
This? This is him?
This is the Great Champion?
This furless, fangless, scale-less, wingless, talonless, shell-less thing? This?

But — the way he fought —
It cannot be. The gods mock us for our hubris. This soft, pink, unprotected thing?

The gods forbade this, Gharta.
Sandorst, you agreed —
The gods forbade this, and you defied them, cozening us into aiding you. And now they have punished us. Mocked us —

No. The spells worked. I felt their strength, all the way through.
We must observe, must learn more. But this is the Great Champion. This is he.

Pff! I won't be responsible.
Not for what happens to you. You brought this on us, "Seeker." You will pay the price.
Oh, we'll all pay the price, Sandorst of Samia. But what that price may be...

Hnh.
Let me through. Let me see the Champion.

He breathes. His heartbeat is steady.
He is just exhausted. Overwhelmed by the transition to the present.
We must –
Study him!
We must read the *auguries!*
Cast his *runes!*
The Champion! The Great Champion! Here among *us!* Did you see how he routed –
The *size* of them! Their weapons! And yet he lit into them like a maddened –

We must get him under cover. And ourselves as well.
Extinguish any fires. Any light at all.

No *fire*? But it's cold —
The bison tribes have fled for now, but they will return, in greater numbers.
They *will* — ?
You are too used to cities, I fear. To being cosseted, protected. We are in the wild world now. Like my home, across the sea.

There are many dangers around us, here and now. And not merely, by any means —

"— THOSE WE HAVE ALREADY *ENCOUNTERED*."

Three

THE NIGHT *PASSED.* WE HEARD THE *GREAT, FLAPPING PASSAGE* OF...ONLY THE GODS KNEW WHAT. AND SOUNDS UTTERLY *ALIEN* TO OUR EARS.
BUT WE *SURVIVED.* COLD AND MISERABLE, WE SURVIVED TO THE *DAWN'S LIGHT.*
AND WHEN WE *DID,* THE GREAT CHAMPION WAS –

WE DIDN'T KNOW *WHAT* HE WAS DOING.

Some... some *questions,* great one.

How do we address you?

And...before we drew you to our time....what did you *do?* It's urgent that we know. What was your *mission?*

The

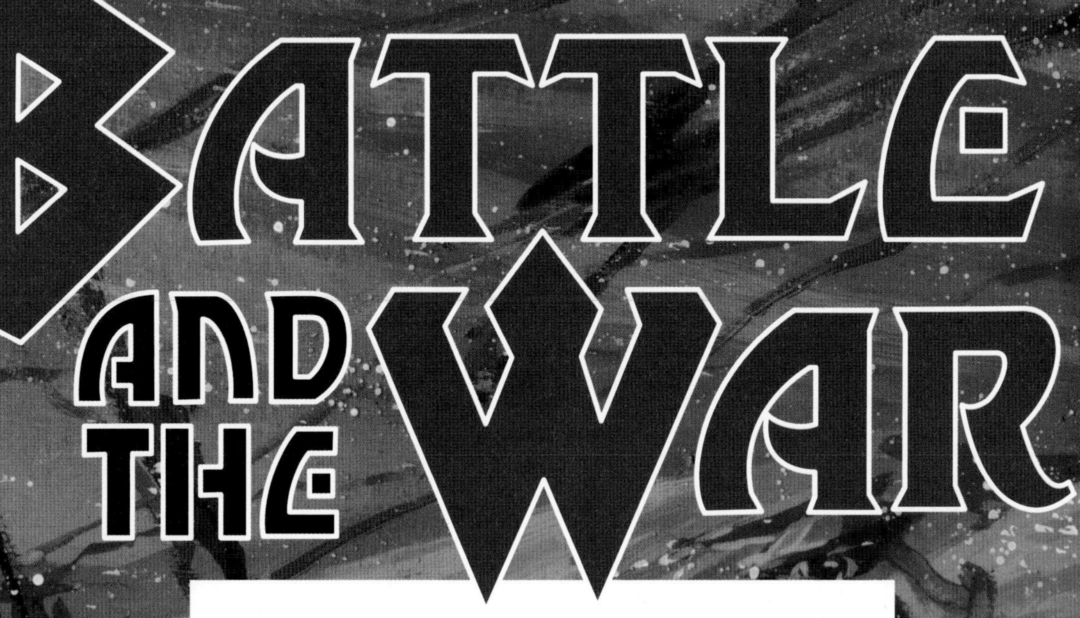

Battle and the War

by NICO BATTANDO

Illustrated by C.C. EMPIK

THE SKIES RIPPED themselves apart with fury, and the noise battered at him like a physical thing. It was constant, deafening—simply too loud for him to feel the cold.

The flat *whramm* of aerial bombardment, the ground shuddering with burst after burst after burst. The whine of pulse-rifles, cycling to intensity between salvos. The tinny bark of commands in his earbug, felt as vibration more than heard. And the screams of the dying.

The walls of the bunker had been breached. The frontal assault was under way. The defenders of the remote base were dug in, well armed—Scramfast ghost troops as well as Kibro soldiers, all ready to die to take Coalition forces with them. They were throwing everything they had into defending the research station.

At least, he hoped it was everything they had.

Whatever it was they were building, whatever esoteric weapon they'd been developing, it could end the war in weeks. So the intelligence boys said, anyway. It had to be taken. Or destroyed.

There was one opening. One slim, billion-to-one shot. The Kyrllic stealth-pods had gotten them this far. And all this hellish noise, all this shattering assault—billions in expense and thousands in lives—was only there to get them a few dekameters further.

The walls of the bunker had been breached. And if he and his hand-picked team could make it in...

L-Learoyd, Steven T.
Master Sergeant, Coalition Forces. You can have my serial number if you want it. There was...a battle...
Yes, yes! *That*, we know!
But we need more. You brought about such *change* — for generations, millennia — and we face such a crisis *now* —

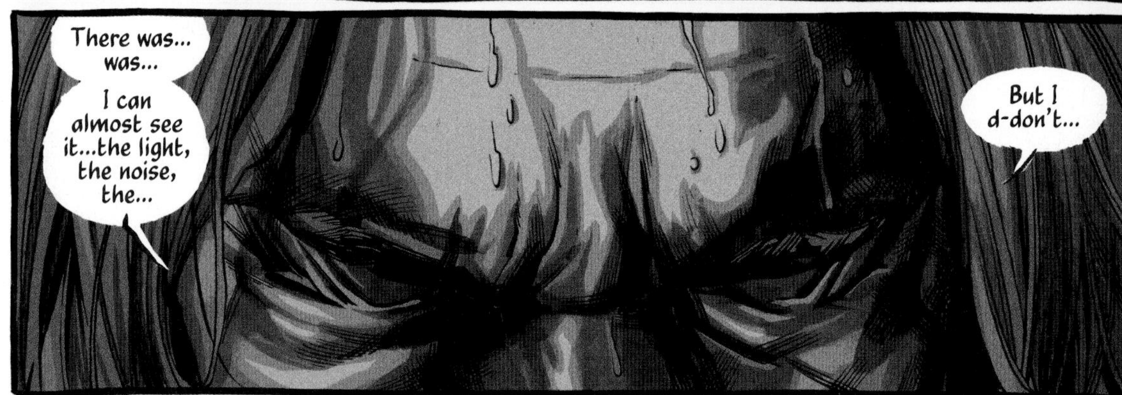
There was... was...
I can almost see it...the light, the noise, the...
But I d-don't...

No. NO!
This is a dream. I'm floating on *Combimorfan* in some field hospital, or delirious from ki-gas burns in a *ditch* somewhere.
Combi... *what?*
A dream?

Craziest fuckin' dream I ever had. What the hell *are* these things?
Eh?
Where does he go?
No, wait —
NOW HOLD ON RIGHT THERE!

Stop right there, Learoyd-Steventy of Coalitia!
I assure you, this is no dream! We have brought you here — at no small amount of expense and sacrifice — to save our world.
We have fed you. Clothed you. And we require some infor—

BACK THE FUCK OFF!
Ah — ah —

Look, Hootie.
I appreciate the pants. But I don't know you. I didn't ask you to bring me here. If here is even anywhere.
I don't even know this isn't some kind of psi-ops clusterfuck, and you're not... not...

Fuck it. I gotta get some air.
Arguing with a goddamn barn owl...

But — but —
Barn owl?

NOT ALL THE WIZARDS OF KENEIL HAD BEEN PART OF GHARTA'S EXPERIMENT.
AND NOT ALL THE SURVIVORS HAD BEEN WIZARDS, EITHER. MANY WERE JUST ORDINARY SOULS.

THEIR HOMES, THEIR LIVELIHOODS DESTROYED, FRIENDS AND FAMILY DEAD –

THEY'D BEEN TOLD IT WAS FOR A GREAT PURPOSE. FOR THE SALVATION OF ALL.
BUT NOW – THEY BEGAN TO WONDER –

Please, gentlebeings. Take heart.
The Great Champion is merely confused.
An aftereffect, perhaps, of the shock of chronal transportation. Give him time. We will talk to him, and –

Ahem I have another item of concern.
Sandorst? This is not the –
Of course it's the time.

Your experiment, Gharta, has ended. Whether this creature you have secured *is* the Champion — or not, as the case may be —
— we have immediate concerns that *must* be addressed.
We are stranded in a crashed city in the Grand Foothills, awaiting a rescue that may *never* come.
We need *organization*, leadership —

And you want to appoint yourself leader.
It's out of the question. We're still in crisis — we need to focus on survival and rescue, not elections and committees. That'll just —
My *dear* wizardess. Need I remind you that I am Third Councillor of Telm?
I daresay I have more experience leading a city population than anyone here.
Oh?

A lot of *wilderness survival issues* in Telm, are there?
I've spent *years* leading teams into the most *hostile regions* of the Autumnlands. This city is *shattered*, and we can't risk —
And who *shattered* it, you puffed-up little nobody? You couldn't lead a *spell-dazzled golem* through an open —

Hey, what's — ?

HALLOOOOOOO!
Hallooo, the city!
My goodness, but you've had an unpleasant time, haven't you? You're supposed to be floating up there among the clouds —
— unless I'm terribly confused.
And I don't think I am.
But allow me to introduce myself. I am Goodfoot. Goodfoot the Trader. Goodfoot the Trusted.
I can scarcely imagine what you've been through. But I swear, whatever I can do to ease your discomforts...I stand ready to help.
At entirely reasonable prices, of course.

Now. I'd like to know what *happened*, of course, but it's *obviously* been traumatic. Perhaps we can just relax and talk...
...over coffee?
Coffee?
Coffee...
Coffee!

AND SO THEY TOLD HER. *ALL* OF IT.
THE SPELL. THE *BACKLASH.* THE ATTACK OF THE *BISON TRIBES.*
AND WHEN THEY WERE *DONE* –

An entire *sky-city,* fallen to ground. An entire city. *Think* of it.
It, ah, must have been *ghastly.* Ghastly...

So. How can I *help?*
Your trade route – when do you next reach tribes that will be in touch with the other sky cities?
We sent a *message spell,* but –

⋛Harrumph⋚ Before we make any further plans, I think we should go through the wreckage more thoroughly.
See what we can salvage, what we have to work with.
Salvage?

All we've recovered since the crash were bare necessities.
We slept on the ground last night. The *ground!* And I don't even want to *discuss* the food.
We have a city here, full of clothing, bedding, food, magic...
The magic is mostly *drained,* Sandorst.
What wasn't lost when the Pattern of Leng ruptured was mostly diverted to the shields, remember?
It cushioned our fall?

We need to focus — on rescue, on the Champion —

Actually, I think Mister Sandorst —
Councillor Sandorst.
— *Councillor* Sandorst has a point. Who knows what we might find that could aid in this crisis?
Surviving medical spells, useful weapons —

Then it's decided. I shall take charge of the salvage efforts. Goodfoot, you can aid me in organizing the work crews.
You, Gharta...

...you keep up your focus on *rescue.* We'll reconvene later, shall we?
I — very well —
Perhaps it'll keep him out of trouble...

WE BEGAN IN *DALLOW'S COURT.* FULL OF HOMES, SHOPS, *STREETS* I'D PLAYED IN ALL MY LIFE.
SOMETIMES THERE WERE *BODIES.* EVERYWHERE THERE WERE *REMINDERS.*

I COULD NOT *IMAGINE* ANYONE LOOKING AT IT AND REMAINING *UNAFFECTED.*
Ah! What a handsome bed! A genuine 10th-era Reverus, if I'm not mistaken. And I am *rarely* mistaken, in such things.
Put that in my *personal* pile, would you?

The *stables!* They did survive — some of them!
Catch them! Catch them! Before —

Sisters both! Of all the things to maintain its magic — !
Well, yes — but if *it* survived, maybe other magic did, too —

Catch it! *Catch it!*

tk

...really must insist, two minutes more rest and then you must get back to...
They're tired, Sandorst. It's understandable.
Here, have a *sea-gem*. A coastal delicacy.
It'll cool you off, restore your energy. They're delicious, too. And don't worry about payment...

..we'll settle up later!

Hnh. We'll eat and sleep better tonight, that's for certain.
That Gharta may not care — she's used to living like the lesser ones, after all. But —
But after this, they'll be eating out of the palm of your hand, Sandorst.

You think so?
I know it. And that makes you the leader I need to deal with.
Go, let them see you leading. We'll... talk later.

Gods of commerce and banking. An entire city. Full of jewellry, trade goods, antiques.
Even if there was no magic at all, it would still be worth it...

oh, the profits to be made, the profits to be made...

Uh-oh. Should we — should we tell Sandorst?
No, not him —

Huh.

A-AAH!

Well, shit.

I hear they're concentrating on salvaging furniture now. Sandorst has an entire study set up for him to relax in.
And won't want to abandon *any* of it, I'm sure.
So. We to stay here?
Looks like we may have –

Uh, Lady Gharta? Seeker?
There's something you should –
Not now, I'm afraid, boys. We just – we have to solve this.

But –
Affa. What do you think?

We setting up barricades. There. And there.
Here too.
And when the bisons they come again –

When the bisons they come again...
Eh?

...you're all going to die.

Oh? And what would you suggest, Mister Learoyd?
Th-the Champion — !

Well, first things first. You gotta get out of here.
It's a city. A little one, but still. You can't possibly block off every goddamn entry point.

Those buffalo-things. When they come back, they'll slip in, spread out —
— and *bam*, you're surrounded.

They'll herd you into the center. That's when the slaughter will start.
Yes, that's what I've been trying to tell them.
So?

So move. But you can't travel with a pack of fuckin' amateurs, not one this big.
Get 'em outta here.
Find a place to stash 'em. Somewhere actually defensible. Send out a messenger to back up that spell you mentioned.

You?
Don't know the territory, don't know the locals. And I'd be better defending the amateurs.

And tell me, Mister Learoyd.
What happened to all this being just a dream?

Maybe it isn't, maybe it is. But if so...
...it doesn't have to be completely damn *stupid*, does it...?
≷hneh≶

This image you're magicking up — can you do one of the whole area?
A map?
Alas, no. To reach out city-wide is a minor thing. To reach for *leagues*, in all directions...
...that requires more power than we currently have.

Okay. I'd have to scout it in person anyway.
Check the terrain, find water, fuel to burn...

They won't agree to go, you know.
Not to begin with, no.
After the first wave of killing, the survivors will change their minds. And that'll be fewer to herd and feed.

You're...very cold, for a hero.
It is what it is.
You can wish real hard it won't happen, or plan for what to do when it does. Your choice.

But if I'm going to scout, I'll need weapons, transportation...
Ah. Now *there*, Mister Learoyd...

"...COUNCILLOR SANDORST'S *SALVAGE OPERATION* CAN ACTUALLY BE *OF USE!*"

Huh.

Most of these look like they're just for show. Silver hilts and fancy inlay, but they'd snap in two in a real fight.

We, ah, don't have many battles in the floating cities.

But the guards on *trading missions* went armed. So..

Ah...

Here...

...*this* is more like it.

Nicely balanced, well-made...
...sturdy enough for action...

...but not heavy.
I like it.

That...that was Red Meg's sword...
A *female's* sword...?
Heh. Quite some Great Champion you've secured for us here, Gharta. I'm eager to see just what he'll do next.
Card tricks? Juggling?
You'd do well, Sandorst, not to chortle too much. *Or too soon.*

Nn. No firearms or grenades. Too bad, but not surprising.
Got a knife, but an extra can't hurt. And maybe a bow...
Ho, furless one.
No wizard am I. Just *Bhord.* Simple *blacksmith,* honest worker. And to me, you look like no *Great Champion.*
You small. Skinny. *Weak.* They say you chase off mess of bison raiders. I do not see this. So I wonder.
You fight them so good —
— you think you fight *me* good, too?

Bhord, was it?
Let me explain something, shithead.
It seems to me you got two possibilities here.
Either I'm not this champion you were hoping for — and whatever was so bad you needed one, you're fucked.
Or I am, and maybe you've got a chance. *Maybe.*
Me, I don't claim I'm any kind of big hero. I'm just what you've got, that's all.
So you can fight me, with my naked skin and my girly sword, and if you win, where are you? Up shit creek without a paddle.
Or *I* win — and *that* wouldn't wind up so well for you either.
You will not — not even turn to *face* me?

Let me ask you something, honest Bhord.
Do you really want me to?

Umm...

Okay. So let's talk about what you furry assholes have by way of transport.
I'm guessing horses are your neighbors and poker buddies...
The *fool.*

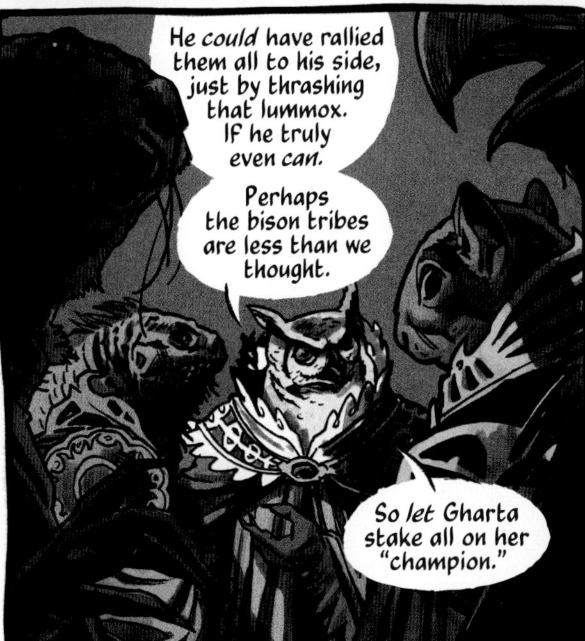
He *could* have rallied them all to his side, just by thrashing that lummox. If he truly even *can.*
Perhaps the bison tribes are less than we thought.
So *let* Gharta stake all on her "champion."

We have an ally who knows the terrain — and understands what's important.
Where *is* Madame Goodfoot, anyway?

Ho, Seven-Scars...
...shall we talk?

Four

WHEN I LEFT, MOST OF THE CITY WAS STILL *ASLEEP.* I DID MY THIRTY-TWO-AND-ONE *OBEISANCES* SWIFTLY AND QUIETLY, AS BEST I COULD, AND CREPT OUT.
AND I REMEMBER *THINKING,* EVEN THEN –

IT WAS THE FIRST TIME I'D EVER LEFT KENIEL ON MY *OWN.*

PELHAU'S CORNER. DALLOWS COURT. *MAGISTER PERRENSON'S* SHOP. MY FATHER'S HOUSE. EVEN AFTER ALL THAT HAD *HAPPENED,* EVEN IN ITS *RUINED STATE* –

– IT WAS STILL *HOME.* THE ONLY ONE I'D EVER KNOWN.

EVERYTHING I'D EVER KNOWN.

A Grand Day Out

by Whittiana Ridar

IT PROMISED TO be a lovely autumnal day; the warm, balmy zephyrs drifted lazily over the pulseless bosom of the nearby river, and whispered low and softly through trembling forest leaves.

All nature was hushed in silence.

But even upon this day the Crookback River was not one of unruffled tranquility, as it coursed southward through the Grand Foothills; for at a point a few miles below Tofar's Plate, a most curious conveyance trotted purposefully through the warming sunshine.

It is with this conveyance that our story opens.

The rider—or perhaps more properly, passenger—of the vehicle, at first glance, would appear indolent, slouched casually among its cushions. But a closer inspection would reveal active, darting eyes that seemingly missed nothing, and a quiet, contained

ILLUSTRATED BY ROGAR

attentiveness that marked all sounds, all smells, even the faint buzz of *squitiria* over the nearby water.

His face, his limbs, revealed little, but his mind recorded much.

Occasionally, his eyes flickered to the sky, as if following a track he saw there, and his mind would direct the tireless limbs of his rude palanquin. And the hilt of his sword was never far from his hand.

He smiled, faintly, as he crested a rise, and took in what lay before him...

IT WAS *ODD*, SEEING THE GREAT CHAMPION RIDE OLD MAGISTER EIKHOUN'S CHAIR. BUT OTHER THAN *THAT*, WE HAD ONLY THE CRICKETS.
HE SAID HE DIDN'T KNOW HOW TO RIDE ONE AND HAD NO TIME TO *LEARN*.

MOST OF THE CITY HAD EXPECTED HIM TO LEAVE ON HIS SCOUTING MISSION *IMMEDIATELY*. BUT HE SAID FIRST LIGHT, AND STUCK *TO* IT.

AND IT WAS GOOD HE *DID*.

THERE'D BEEN NO FURTHER *ATTACKS* FROM THE BISON TRIBES. SO SOME THOUGHT THEY WERE *SAFE*, AND COULD WHILE AWAY THE NIGHT IN *COMFORT* –

SKREEE SKREEEEEE

AHH!

AAAAHHHHH!

IF HE HADN'T *BEEN* THERE –
SKRII?
HRAA!

HNAAA!
SKKH!
NO!
No! Please –

SKIHHH*
Eh?

Under cover! Get the fuck under cover, you morons!
Nnh!

WE *DID* –

AND *MORE* –

BUT I FEAR THEY WOULD HAVE *KEPT COMING*, IF NOT FOR –
SKAAAAAAAAA

SK-KK
H-nhh!

Huh.
Bats.

NOT THAT THAT *ENDED* MATTERS –
...said you'd keep us *safe*, Seeker! You said you knew how to *survive* down here on the ground!
If you can't –
I *also* said not to light any fires.
What do you think *that* says, to the wild predators of the night? "Nothing to see here? Move *along*?"
Well, if you can't get them to obey *you*, Gharta –
And who gave them the *liquor*, Sandorst? Ardunn's *eyes*, it's like you *want* to be –
What about the *rescue beacon*? When will they –
– *Champion?* All he has to do is *restore magic*, and we can –
– *cold!* This is intolerable –
Now, wait a – you've got to have – can't just –
⁼ sigh ⁼
I WONDERED HOW THEY COULD *BADGER* AT HER LIKE THAT –

– BUT I BEGAN TO WONDER ABOUT THAT *RESCUE BEACON*, TOO.
Hey, kid –
– c'mon out.
It's hard enough keeping an eye on you *and* paying attention to the terrain in front of me.
H-*huh?*
Those fuckin' bats we tangled with are already home licking their wounds, but they won't have been the whole colony.
And if I can spot a straggler or...ah.
That – that's *them!*
But...why do you want to know where the bats *live*, Great One?
You need to ride on the chair, too? I think it can carry us both.
But I've got a lot of ground to cover today, and if I have to wait for you...

Hah. I'm a terrier, sir.
I ran this chair down yesterday. I can outrun it all day if I need to.
Well, okay. Then let's see what you can do, terrier.
I DIDN'T KNOW WHAT HE WAS LOOKING FOR. I BARELY KNEW WHAT HE WAS LOOKING AT.
JUST THAT WHATEVER IT WAS, I WANTED TO SEE IT TOO.
SO I RAN, AND LOST MYSELF IN RUNNING. AND MY WORRIES FELL AWAY, AT LEAST FOR A TIME. MY FATHER, THE CITY, THE DANGER, ALL OF IT –
– LEFT BEHIND IN THE BREEZE.
Um, Great One? Can I ask you a question?
Enough with this goddamn "Great One." Call me Learoyd.
Really? I mean... really?
Spit it out.

You're not of any tribe I ever heard of. Not a dog, not a bird, not even an ape from across the seas.
What... are you?
Huh. I guess that makes sense, in this weird-ass world. No people, just animals.

No, we're all peop –
I'm a man, kid. A human being.
A *yumanbein*? What's that?
It's... well, it's...

DA!
DADDEE!

Maybe nothing that even matters any more.
If this *isn't* a dream. If I really am in some fucked-up future where everything I remember's...

Look, kid, what's your name again?
Dunstan. Dunstan Dourlainson.
Sounds kinda blue-blood. Your friends call you that?
They, uh, call me Dusty.

Okay. Then let's quit jabbering and move out.
Sound good, Dusty?

WE RANGED FAR AND WIDE, *UP* THE RIVER AND DOWN. HE SEEMED MOST INTERESTED IN THAT ONE *CLIFF*, AND IN THE RIVER ITSELF.
BUT THAT WAS NOT *ALL* –

Um, sir?
L-Learoyd?
Shhh!

Hear 'em rustling around in there?
They're not asleep any more. They must sleep in the mornings, after their nightly hunts. But by this late in the day...

Y-yes, sir.
But... why do you need to...?
This way.

Hm.
It oughtta be...
There.
Take a look. But stay quiet.

That – that's where they live? The bison tribe?
But –
But my father said –
Their beasts. They're thin. Unhealthy. And where are all the –
Dusty –

HRAAAAA-
H-hrf?
Their women are out gathering plants, what there is still available. I spotted a few. The kids are watching over the tribe's animals.
What I'd like to know is, where are the goddamn *men*? The adult males? Haven't seen any...
This was...he was just a child? And you killed him?
He'd have killed *you* without fuckin' thinking twice.
It's a dangerous world, kid. Any world, it seems. You gotta know what's out there that can hurt you. You gotta be prepared to act.

Um.
I think... I think there's something I should tell you. About danger out there.
About Sandorst the Exacting. And that coyote trader, Goodfoot...

Ahh, thank you very much... Rion, was it? Your hard work is most appreciated.
You may go now.

Hmm. Still decent thaumatic charge in the crystal. Double-fretted for capacity, even.
And a Ring of Delira's Amorous Wonder. Quite nice craftsmanship, too...

Salvage going well, Sandorst?
I spotted some very fine vintages, in the brandies you've stored in the back.
I confess, Madame Goodfoot, I am, ah, a bit discomfited. You see...

...none of these items, taken alone, have a great deal of magic left to them at all. But together?
They might be enough to power another message beacon. Should we really be hiding them?
Hnh.

Please. You'd hand them over to Gharta, let *her* seize all the credit when you've done the work?
When you bring the survivors home, safe and sound after her disastrous "experiment," will you be Third Councillor then?
Or something more?
Well. I suppose...

Of course. Now go. Let them see how busy you are. How hard you work for them.
And later, we'll talk about the next steps in dealing with Gharta.
Indeed...

Not a great deal of magic? Not to a wizard, perhaps.
But in the Principates, sold on the right markets? I could live like a queen. It'll be tricky, so tricky...

No *attack*?
Let them *live*? But –

Hush, Seven-Scars. You'll want to let them live anyway.
The Cities will forgive you *some* payback. But you don't want to make them *too* mad.
I'll let you know when it's safe. When you can take down their fabled warrior without trouble.

And then you can loot the city for its treasures. Shackle the populace, ransom them for a fortune.
And their magic. We take their magic for *our own.*

Ah, yes. *Certainly!*
A city like this, it must be *rich* in magic. Magic everywhere. And it'll be yours, all you can *find* —

You talk like *serpent*, coyote.
But you spin happy lies to *them*, yes? Not to Seven-Scars. Not to Seven-Scars, or —
No, *no!* Of course not —

Yes, tricky...

...but do-able...
Yes, Dame Hornsworth. *Finest* we've found.
Saved it for you special.
Ale?
Ah!

Lady Gharta! Lady Affa! Care to join us?
I know you work hard keeping us safe, but a full belly has its value, too...
Thank you, Councillor Sandorst...

...but I think not today.
And please do not give too much ale or brandy out to any *one group*, if you'd be so kind.
It may not be what you've saved for yourself, Sandorst. But it can still addle minds.

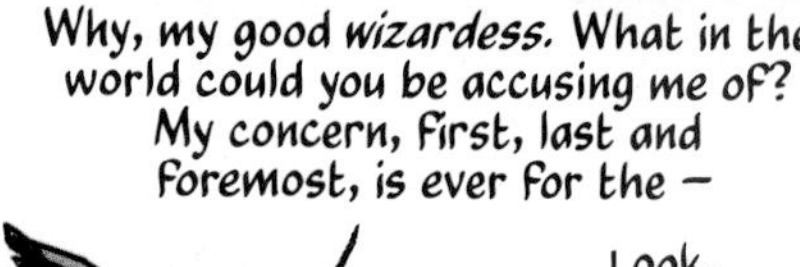
Why, my good *wizardess*. What in the world could you be accusing me of? My concern, first, last and foremost, is ever for the –

Look, *look!*

The Great Champion's back!

Dusty! I couldn't find you this morning! I didn't know you'd –
It's okay, I'm fine –
Dusty –
Enna! What are you *doing?* Come over here at once, young –
Gharta. Let's talk.

...right over the bridge. It's a good area to hole up. Plenty of water, plenty of fuel. We can hunt, build shelters, wait out the rescue there.

And if there's an attack...

..we just destroy the motherfucking bridge. Strand 'em on the opposite bank. No other way to cross for miles in either direction.

Mm.

It looks good, Mr. Learoyd. Except...we don't have enough stored magic to destroy the bridge.
We could gather it, but it would take some time.

Yeah. I'm workin' on that. Speaking of which...

Goodfoot!
Hey, Goodfoot!
Hm?
Just the coyote-gal I wanted to see! Let's talk about what you've got for sale...

Brimstone? Certainly I have some. Finest in the plains. The fumes are ideal for pest control, and it's used in some salves and balms.
Sandorst has *more*, since it's a wizardly staple. But I couldn't guarantee the quality.

I'll take all you've got. How about string? Some sort of fine string?
Finest hemp cord. Miles of it, the best you'll find anywhere.
But, ah, sir, why would you...?

Will this cover it?
Ah... ah...

I need your help with something else, too. Something serious.
I need you to talk to the bison...
What? *Me?!* You think that *I'd* ally myself with –

Well, you're a trader, right? You trade *with* the plains tribes...?
Oh! Oh, yes, of *course!*
I know the bison tribes, of course. And their current leader. Seven-Scars, I believe his name is, but I'm not certain...

I need to arrange a parley with him. The two of us, face to face.
A parley?

I thought you were the Champion? You can't just...conquer them? With your sword of lightning?
Ha. Not as fuckin' easy as all that.
Plus, I'm not Superman. I took 'em by surprise, last time, in the dark. Next time, it might not go so good.

North of here. There's, like, a circle, a flat stone. You know it?
Tofar's Plate? Near the cliffs?
That's the one. It'd be perfect. If you can set up a parley, a few *days* from now...

THEY TALKED FOR *SOME TIME.* AND MORE AND MORE, GOODFOOT *SMILED...*

THAT NIGHT IN THE CITY WAS *DIFFERENT.*
THERE WERE NO FIRES. NO *CAROUSING.* ANY DRINKING WAS DONE IN PRIVATE.

SANDORST'S MEN HAD CLEARED OUT *ROOMS.* FOUND BLANKETS, BEDDING.
A *GUARD* WAS SET, WATCHING THE SKIES.

BUT I COULDN'T *SLEEP.*
I'D TOLD HIM GOODFOOT WAS OUT TO LOOT THE CITY. AND HE'D GONE RIGHT TO HER. *CONFIDED* IN HER. WAS HE TRULY ON OUR SIDE? WAS HE *TRULY* THE GREAT –
Hey, Dusty...

L-L-LEAROYD!

...just the terrier I wanted to *see.* I could use a little help.

Interested?

Five

HE ASKED FOR MY HELP. SO OF *COURSE* I GAVE IT TO HIM.
AND I ASKED *OTHERS*, AS WELL. IT WOULD BE A *GRAND ADVENTURE*, I THOUGHT.
IF OUR PARENTS HAD KNOWN, THEY WOULD *SURELY* HAVE FORBIDDEN IT. THOSE OF US WHO STILL *HAD* PARENTS.
BUT THAT WAS PART OF THE *THRILL*. A SECRET MISSION. AT THE BEHEST OF THE *GREAT CHAMPION*.
A MISSION INTO DANGER. INTO DEADLY SURROUNDINGS...
Whoaaaa.
Th-this is it? It's chilly. I w-wouldn't have expected it to be —
Shhhh. Quietly. Very quietly. Don't even knock over a rock. You can do that, right?
Okay, good. Then let's go...

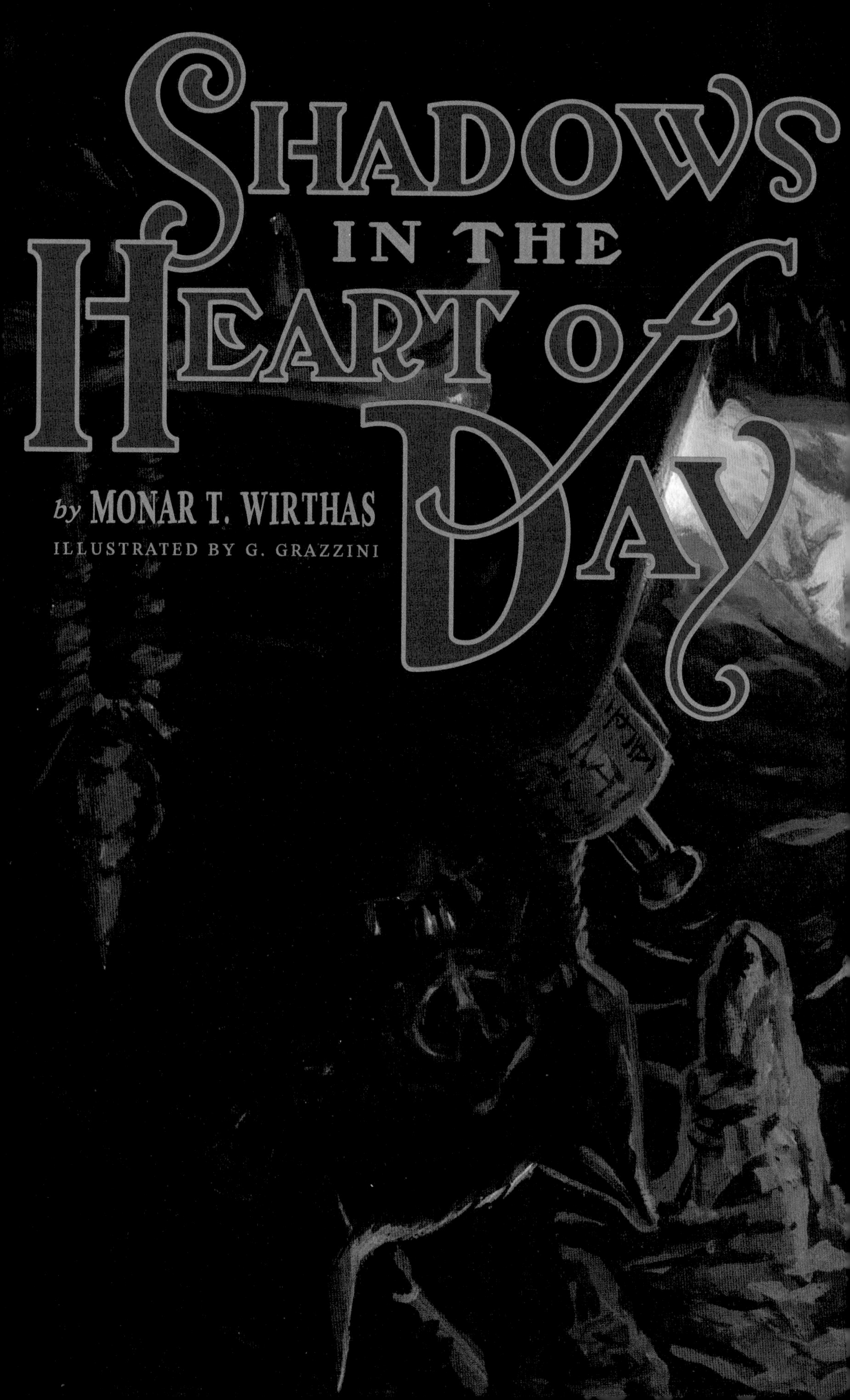

Shadows in the Heart of Day

by MONAR T. WIRTHAS

ILLUSTRATED BY G. GRAZZINI

HROTAKH, CLAN HUNT leader and veteran of uncounted battles, shifted and snarled uneasily in his slumber.

The night's hunt had gone poorly. The new place, wooden and falsestone and broken, redolent with the scent of used magic, had proved disappointing. Those within had learned to hide at night, to huddle away from sky. The huntflyers could hear their steady breathing, their hearts pumping rich blood, but could not reach them. Not without forcing themselves through narrow ways that entangled wings. And that, Hrotakh would not allow. He remembered their blades, especially that of the fierce one who took five of his best. Five brave hearts who would never soar again. Or hear the echoes of their keening calls off stone and leaf and water.

Hrotakh felt their loss, and a seething anger at the fierce one who had stilled them.

There were takings, of course. Shell-crawlers and riverbankers and even a stray woolly buck from the grunters' herds. But they had hoped for a feast, felt it close and succulent, and had been denied.

And now something was wrong. The smells, the sounds. So like the fierce one, and those he guarded. It was a dream, a sour dream.

Hrotakh twitched his teeth and tongue and muttered unformed curses...

Ghahh! Get away from me with that –
THE MISSION, ONCE WE LEARNED IT, WAS REPELLENT.
Bat guano? But why do we need –
Ha! Don't slip, Reg! Don't slip, or you'll be all-over...
HRNH...
HRFFL...
BUT THE DANGER –
Uh...
– THE DANGER WAS REAL AS COULD BE.
Okay, that oughtta be enough. Time to go. And don't wake anyone up.
Quietly, quietly...
IT MAKES MY FUR CRAWL TO THINK HOW EASILY IT COULD HAVE GONE WRONG.
BUT IT FELT GOOD. I DIDN'T KNOW WHAT WE'D DONE –

– BUT DOING *ANYTHING* FELT GOOD, AT THAT POINT.

Ha ha ha! Want some? Want some?

Nooooooooo...

WE GOT BACK WITHOUT BEING *MISSED.*

BUT THEN, THERE WERE *OTHER* THINGS GOING ON –

Lady Gharta? Lady Affa?

In the name of the *Grand Council* and the authority of the Seventeen Cities, as the *highest-ranking* official available...

What in...?

...I hereby declare that you are being placed *under arrest,* for actions endangering the *lives* of the Citizenry.

Arrest? Stop talking nonsense, Sandorst!
We have important work to do if any of us are to survive!
Stop playing games and –
No games, Seeker.

You'll be confined and guarded, treated with the honor due your stature as wizards, until such time as a tribunal may be convened.
We're going to have order once more, and proper leadership.
And as for that so-called legendary *thug* of yours —

Learoyd!
Ahh!
This looks a little more...military than things were yesterday. What's goin' on, Hootie? Coup d'etat Tuesday?
You'd be well advised, "Great One"...

...not to meddle in matters that don't concern you!
Javv's Stunning Bolts!
=hnh=

Ah...
...the hell?
Now *that's* interesting. Javv's Bolts, you said?

Silence! You are under arrest, Seeker! You may not *speak!*
Your focus-crystal is to be *impounded!*

As for you, Mister Learoyd, that...was just a warning!
If you value your hide, unprotected as it is — you won't interfere further.

Ehh.
None of my fuckin' business how you guys run things. Coups, pogroms, jousts, limbo contests...it's no skin off my nose.
What?

Then come along, Seeker. Come along.
We've fitted out quite a tidy little cell for the two of you. I expect you'll find it most comfortable...
But —

Huh.

I don't — I don't understand.
He wants a parley, our little Champion does. To meet you on neutral ground, talk some sort of bargain. He's even picked out the spot.
I told him I'd bring you his request.
Parley? Why he want parley, Goodfoot? What is purpose?
Is trick?
Oh, I doubt that.
I expect he has something terribly heroic in mind. Single combat, most likely. You against him, for the lives of the sky-dwellers.
It's how heroes think, isn't it?
No. No fight solo.
He small, but fast. Good fighter. We strong, but we make war rarely. When we do, we crush with numbers.
Why Seven-Scars agree to such a thing?

I didn't say you should agree to it. Oh, no.
Let him think you're going to. Discuss the rules. But don't actually agree to anything.

And then...
...when you've got him out there...
...away from the city...

Well, *you* know Tofar's Plate.
You know how the hillside dips, right at the base of the cliff. All along the base. Why, you could fit an army in there...

...and no one up at the Plate would even see it...
Ahhh. Is good, is *good!*
You tell champion we parley *tomorrow.*

Not tomorrow, no. Let's say...three days. We set it up for three days from now.
Three days? But...
Don't want to appear too eager, make him start *thinking* about things....
Hnh.

Besides...
...a girl does need a little time to finish looting a city of its magic and jewelry, and to get out...

I don't like it, no. I don't like it at all.

A negotiation? With our besiegers? In his hands? It depends too much on him, and I don't trust him. Or understand him.
Look, Sandy, it's really not such a —
Councillor Sandorst, trader. Or "Your Grace," if you prefer.

And I still don't like it. My magic — Javv's Bolts didn't work on him. Why? I had enough power.
That...was troubling.
Did the spell fail?
No. I felt it — it worked properly.

But there's something about him...
...is it possible he really is the Champion?

Oh, *tosh.*
You're as nervous as a one-legged stork making his way through a gopher field, Councillor.
Let him play. It keeps him occupied, and gives us time to gather more magic.

Your salvage crews are still working, aren't they?
Hm? Well, yes, of course. But I don't know how much more there is to find. And really, how much do we need?

You want to find every speck.
You want to make sure that when you call for a rescue, it comes. That *you* are the hero of the day. Otherwise...
Otherwise? Otherwise what?

Otherwise, there's a lot of blame to go around, your Grace. And the story they'll listen to...
...it'll be the one that sounds best.

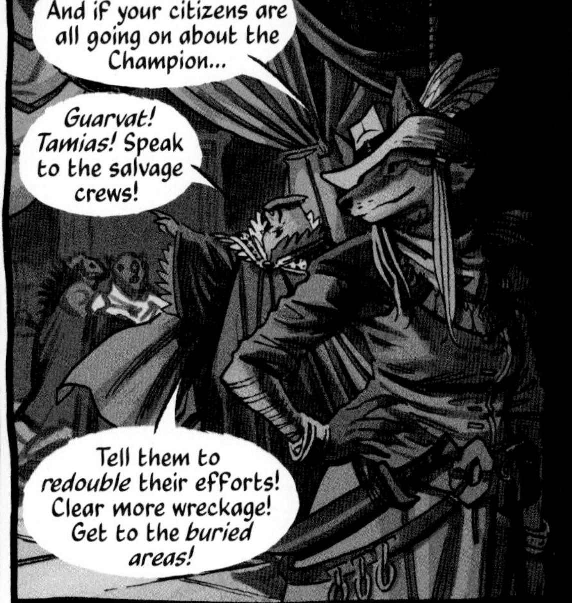
And if your citizens are all going on about the Champion...
Guarvat! Tamias! Speak to the salvage crews!
Tell them to *redouble* their efforts! Clear more wreckage! Get to the *buried areas!*

Huh.
You, ah...do have a plan, right?
I think... I think Sandorst's dangerous.

You liked coming along this morning, didn't you? Being part of it.
Um... *yes!*

It just...there's so much I don't know. So much I can't control. Having something to do, even a little thing...

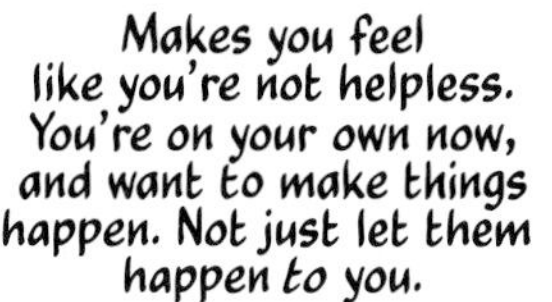

Makes you feel like you're not helpless. You're on your own now, and want to make things happen. Not just let them happen *to* you.

That's good. Keep thinkin' that way.
hiiiih...

AND IT WASN'T UNTIL AFTER HE WAS *GONE* THAT I REALIZED –

– HE HADN'T ANSWERED MY *QUESTION.* THAT HE ALMOST NEVER *DID.*

You mentioned another message spell. You think that's the way to go? To call to the other cities, rather than act on our own?

I leave that entirely to you, your Grace.

A message, a spell that bends the bison to your will...a sunblasted levitation spell that puts this city afloat again. It doesn't matter.

Just so long as it's spectacular, and all yours.

You prepare, Councillor. Gather the magic to power whatever it is you do, and prepare. I'll tell you when the time is right.

Yes, yes...

THE NEXT *MORNING* –
GAD'S WHARF HAD *BROKEN FREE,* FALLEN AWAY FROM THE REST OF KENIEL. BUT IT HAD BEEN A CLUSTER OF *MANUFACTURIES* –

– AND MUCH *EQUIPMENT* STILL REMAINED THERE, IN WORKING ORDER.
THE CHAMPION – LEAROYD – SPENT A GREAT DEAL OF *TIME* THERE –
Okay, okay...
...soaked for a day. Ready to filter it, get the potassium nitrate out, start another load.
What next?
tek
Yeah, yeah...
Pulverize it once it's dry, mix with the alder charcoal, sulfur and additives...

A DAY. THEN *TWO* –

Hnh. Can't direct the blast well, even with what field enhancements I can add in a place like this. But properly placed, maybe...

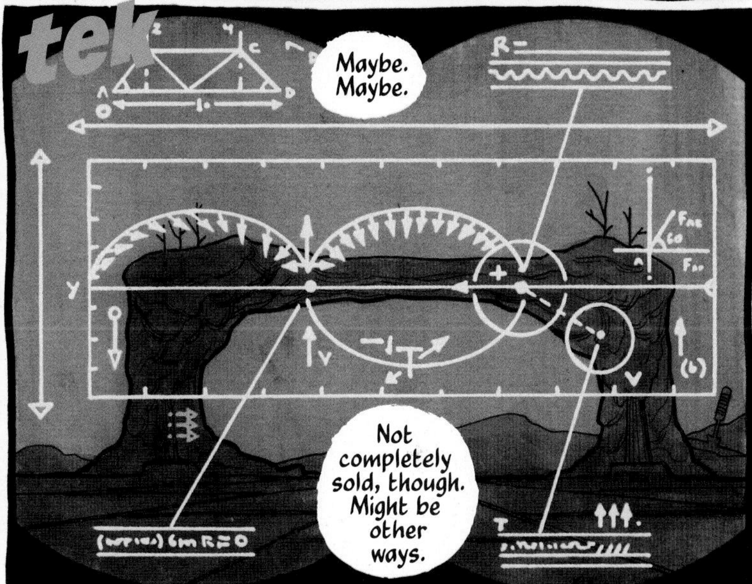
tek
Maybe. Maybe.
Not completely sold, though. Might be other ways.

And she wasn't kidding about having miles of this, was she? Hope it'll be enough.

Soak it in the solution...

It will be all right, Gharta. You have been in worse straits, and navigated them unscathed.

You will sail clear of this, as well.

Ah, Affa. My ever-faithful Affa. I have dragged you so *far,* all these years.

Around the world and back again, and then off anew…

You have dragged me nowhere, dearest. Everywhere you have gone…

…I have *wanted* to be there with you.

I only worry…

Locked up as we are, when the danger comes... you may be killed too.
A risk I accepted long ago. Without you...

Ladies!
And how are we today?!
Hm?

Enjoying the accommodations, I trust?
We had to *reinforce* them here and there, but altogether, I think it'll keep out the wind and rain, eh?
You're being played for a fool, Sandorst. Even you have to recognize that.

The bison tribes are as great a threat as ever, and as for the coyote... she only wants coin, and as much of it as she can carry.
You have to stop this. Before it's too late.

Really, Gharta. I wouldn't have thought you to be quite so transparent. You've been outmaneuvered. It happens to...
...well, to *most*, in politics, over time. Accept it gracefully.
Gods of education and welfare! These are *lives* you're throwing away, Sandorst! Your own daughter –

I'll have some wine sent over, shall I? Not the best vintage, but beggars can't be choosers, hm?
You won't see anything as good once you're locked up in the Cities above, I daresay...

That...*fool!* That utter, unmitigated, *cack-brained* –
Gharta. Calm yourself. You'll burst a blood vessel.
Repeat the three koans. We can do it together, all right?

You all right in there?

Learoyd?
Don't worry about Sandorst. He's an asshole, but there are always assholes. Anywhere. Any*time*, even, it seems.
At least they're dependable, even if you can only count on them to be so shit-stupid they can't see straight.

LEAROYD!
Get a rope! A ladder, *anything!* Get us *out* of *here!*

No, no...
You're safer in here. At least for now.
What?!

LEAROYD! OH, YOU'RE AS BAD AS THE REST OF THEM!
Gharta! Gharta, my love, please –
LEAROYD!

YOU COME BACK HERE RIGHT NOW! I'LL GREAT CHAMPION YOU, YOU JUMPED-UP, HAIRLESS –
Gharta – !

I *LOST* HIM, AS HE CLAMBERED AROUND THE CITY, VISITING THIS PLACE AND THAT.
BUT AS EVENING FELL, HE REACHED *GAD'S WHARF* AGAIN.

WHAT HE MIGHT BE *DOING,* THOUGH –

WHERE DID HE *GO?* I DIDN'T KNOW, NOT THEN.
TO THE *CLIFFS?*

TO THE *BRIDGE?*
WHAT DID HE *THINK* ABOUT? THE AUTUMNLANDS? THE WORLD ENTIRE?

THE WORLD HE *CAME* FROM? HOW IT HAD CHANGED?
I DIDN'T *KNOW.* NOT THEN. I DIDN'T KNOW.

THERE WAS SO MUCH I DIDN'T KNOW –
It's the right move. I know it is.
But perhaps the warthog is right, and Goodfoot's playing a game of her own.
Wouldn't do to underestimate her.
She's been nothing but helpful...

And who does that?
That's when you've got to watch extra-closely...

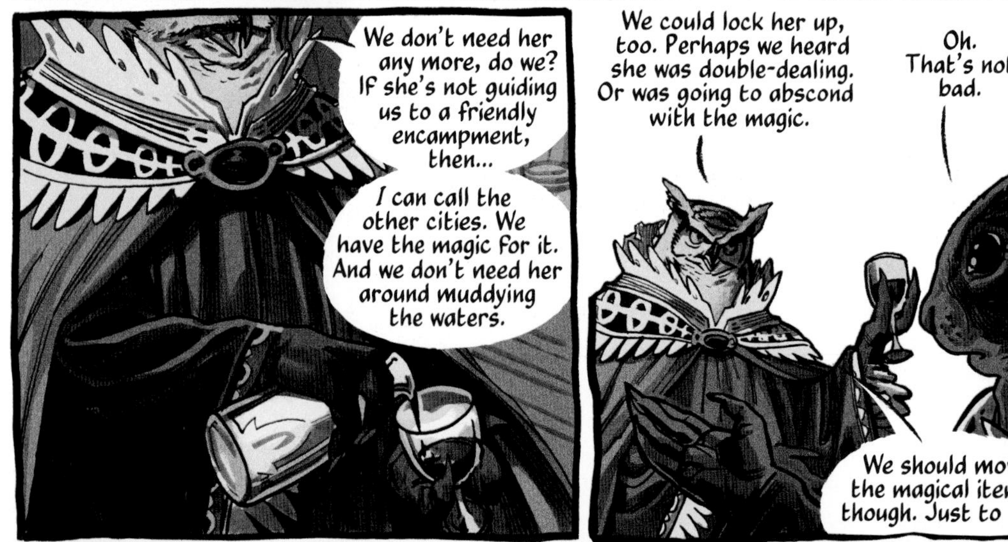
We don't need her any more, do we? If she's not guiding us to a friendly encampment, then...
I can call the other cities. We have the magic for it. And we don't need her around muddying the waters.
We could lock her up, too. Perhaps we heard she was double-dealing. Or was going to abscond with the magic.
Oh. That's not bad.
We should move the magical items, though. Just to be –

WHERE IS IT?!

Where is...what? Really, Madame Goodfoot —
The *magic*, you *feathered fool!*
I went to...to *check* on it, to make sure all was in readiness, and it's gone!
Did you move it? *Secrete* it somewhere?

I...*of course not!* Why would I?
It's really gone?
Like it was never *there.* Come and see.

This is — it — it —
All your salvage. All the stored magic — crystals, rings, everything. The money, too. Everything small and portable of any value.
You didn't do this?

What do you *think* of me, madame?

It's just — we need to act *now!* Tonight!
The parley is tomorrow. If we haven't made our move by then —

"– THEN IT'S ALL IN THE CHAMPION'S HANDS –"
There. In hiding.
Be ready.
And make no sound.

Six

THE DAY OF THE PARLEY DAWNED *POORLY* –

Rain. Yeah, like that's something we fuckin' need today.
If it holds off a few hours, maybe...

I HAD DONE MY DAILY *OBEISANCES*, BUT I QUICKLY ADDED ANOTHER –
Natawis, guardian of the weather, grandchild of Tofar, look kindly on what we do this day...

FOR THE *GREAT CHAMPION* HAD A PLAN TO SAVE US ALL. I DID NOT KNOW WHAT IT *WAS* –
– BUT I KNEW HE HAD A *PLAN* –

– AND IT *MUST* SUCCEED.
Hey. Hey, kid –
– get a move on, willya? I need to check the site.

IDENTE'S

PROMISE

by DOLIAN
4th REVEN ACOLYTUS

For I say to thee, keep clean in thy ways and true to thy gods, and surely they will light thy path and smite those who transgress against thee."

— The Book of Idente, 4:13:33

Words every child knows from cradle-time. Words we aspire to, though we too often fail. But words, nonetheless, that are not mere hope. No. They are a covenant, a sacred promise.

Warriors and holy fools, rulers and beggars, the lost and the mighty, all hear the promise. And those who believe, they are the blessed.

It was a day of glory, in the Grand Foothills, where a momentous meeting unfolded and Idente's Promise was shown once more to all who might see. Picture it. Warm sun, gentle breezes, the slightest taste of winter on the air.

Picture it, and hold it in your heart: At Tofar's Plate—the Great Champion stands, his brow unlined, his face at peace. His bearing noble and handsome, his belief strong. The folk of the Broken City behind him, trusting their lives to his protection. And facing them, the hordes of the Renegade, in their thousands. Scarred, glowering, twisted by both birth and nature. Rank upon rank of them, eager for blood. Muttering unholy curses and shaking their thirsty blades.

But does the Champion shrink from them? No.

ILLUSTRATED BY THE OTOPA BROTHERS

HE APPROACHED ALONG A *DIFFERENT PATH* FROM THE USUAL. CAST HIS EYES IN ALL *DIRECTIONS*, SNIFFED THE AIR AS IF THERE WAS SOMETHING TO *SMELL* –

Man, I don't like that sky.

Look, kid, I need to ask you something. I've done everything I can, but there are no guarantees in life...

...and we might need some backup.

Yes. Anything.

If need be, can you quickly light a fire?
HAH!
I'm a wizard's pup. I haven't had my full training, yet...
...but fire is the second spell we learn, after light.

Well. Okay, then.
Listen close. I think we're all right here, but I need to tell you about the bridge. And if necessary, you can tell Gharta...

IN THE CITY, EVERYONE *PREPARED* FOR THE PARLEY.
ALMOST EVERYONE –
By the *two-headed goddess,* where in blazes is it?
What – what are you doing?
Magical items leave traces, Goodfoot. A ghost of themselves, a shadow where they lay. A skilled wizard can *trace* magic.
I should be able to track it, to sense the hand of whoever took it, but...

Ah. Got away clean, hm?
Well, then, I wish you all the best...
...but a girl's got to know when to cut her losses. I'll pack up my goods, and...

...eh?
What *is* this? Surely you – ah – have no complaint with –

I think you'll stay, Madame.
You orchestrated this "parley," and have had *great interest* in our salvaged treasures. I think you'll see it all out with us.

Sandorst! Let us out! Surely even *you* can't be such an utter ninny as to –
Pff. The prisoners.

This is your doing, warthog. *All* your doing, trying to subvert the proper authority of the city!
Don't come crying to *me* for mercy!

Fah.
We *must* get out. Affa, is there any chance?
Um...
Even if we use everything, I doubt it'll come close...

AND THE TIME *CAME.*
AND *WE* CAME, AS WELL, TO OBSERVE. *GENTLEBEINGS* AND WORKERS, THE YOUNG AND THE *OLD* –

AND THE SKIES CONTINUED TO *DARKEN* –

RRRMMBBLL

Great...
Uh -

Ho, "Champion." Seven-Scars is here for parley.

AND I *KNEW*. HE HAD A PLAN.
Okay, kid. I got this. Get back with the others.

HE WAS THE *GREAT CHAMPION,* AND HE HAD A PLAN.

Seven-Scars, right? And honked off, I bet. Can't really blame you, the way you've been treated.

But you fight for them.

I do. This is the side I'm on.

Is wrong side.

Maybe. But it's the side I'm on.

A lot of them are assholes. But not all of them. They don't deserve what you want to do to them.

Hnh.

So you fight for them.

No one fight for us but us.
Yeah. That can be a problem.
So how you save them? Single combat?
Would that work?
I think no.
Kinda what I thought, too.
So...what is parley for?
Honestly? Mostly just to delay you.
Delay? Until what?
The cliff over there? There's an upside-down bucket on top, braced with stones to keep it from blowing away.
Under the bucket, safe from the wind, is a candle. It's been burning down for a few hours.
If I've timed it right...the candle-flame ought to hit the fuse in just a few more —

WHOOM
KOOM
KOOM
KROOM

WE HAD NO IDEA WHAT HAD JUST *HAPPENED.* THE SOUND. THE *GROUND* SHAKING. WE DIDN'T COMPREHEND.

VVHRMMMMMMM

NOT UNTIL WE BEGAN TO HEAR THE *SCREAMING* –

Huh. Candle must have burned faster than I thought. Or the fuse –
You...do this?
You... you...
Hnh...
Nnh...
– you
MONSTER!
You break rules of parley!
Says the guy who hid a fuckin' bison army at the base of a cliff, pal. Besides, we never agreed on any –
RRRRAAAHHHHH!
htt –

What did he –
That – was not magic, but –
He – *killed* them?
Dozens – scores of them?
Like a wild animal –
Vicious –
Vile –
Pretty clever, actually –
But –
HE'D HAD A *PLAN.* I'D *KNOWN* HE HAD A PLAN. BUT –
Dusty! Go!
You know what *to do!*
Killed – he just killed all of –
GO!

The rest of you! Don't go back to the city! Get over the bridge to the other side of the river!
The rockfall won't have gotten all of them —
RUUUU-
— and they'll be fuckin' pissed!
Bhord! You and your pals, you're armed! Stick with me — we need a rear guard to watch everyone's back while they —
Uh?
Us?
Hnh?
Great. Nice to have dependable help.

Ah, well.
We'll just have to make do with what we've got.
AND SO THE PARLEY ENDED.
MOST OF US RAN.
A FEW OF US STOOD.
AND THE STORM –
– THE STORM BROKE.

I DID AS THE CHAMPION *ASKED*. I REACHED THE CITY –
≈nnh! hnhh!≈ Almost –
Gharta! Lady *Gharta!* I've come to get you out!
Give me a minute to get the *door!*
Oh, thank the gods of home and hearth.
That sounds *much* safer...
I TOLD THEM WHAT HAD *HAPPENED* –
What? He did *what?!*
Of all the insane, *violent* – what is he, an uncivilized *beast?* They could have been reasoned with! *Bargained* with! If only I hadn't been –
≈*sigh*≈ Never mind. What's done is done.
Rally all those who stayed behind. Get them to the bridge.
Right away!

THEY DID NOT *WANT* TO GO.
BUT WHEN WE TOLD THEM SANDORST WAS *ALREADY* HEADED FOR THE BRIDGE...
Sandorst? The Councillor from Telm?
Who organized the salvage teams?

AS IF HE'D HAVE GIVEN THEM A *SECOND THOUGHT.*

AND WHEN WE GOT THERE –
There! There they *are!* But –
Run! Run, you *fools!*
They're close *behind* us!

BUT THE *RIVER* –
GO! GO!
THE RIVER WAS *BAD* –

Nice work, Bhord! Keep it up!
He's exposed, Arkan! Make him pay!

Undignified –
Not proper for city officials to be made to –
The magic! With the storm – it's hard to focus –
But I can sense it –
– the stolen magic! It's here, somewhere!
Hm?

...there, you woolly-faced cocksucker!
I think that's the last of them!

No, killer-of-dozens...
...not the last.
You murder my tribe. My brothers. Kill with trick, not even face in combat.
You foul. Lower than the lowest creatures...
...and you die for this.
Sir? We can —
No. Get Gutruk across. Get him to help, he earned it.
I'll be right behind you.

Quick now.
I don't have much room to...

...maneuver here!

What, killer? No so *savage* now?
Don't need to be, shaggy.
No one waiting in *ambush* now, is there?

Quick – we need a healer for –
Oh, no! *Look!*

CUT THEM ALL DOWN!

Htah!

Dusty! Blow the bridge! Now!

RHAHHA!
Dammit, Dusty, do it! For fuck's sake, they'll kill you all!

The magic! It's close — I can feel it! Tap into it —
Please, no! I c-can't...

Oh!
Look, look!
Oh, praise the gods, praise the gods...

...we're saved!
Rescue! Rescue at last!

No.
They won't get here and find him being the hero. No. I won't —

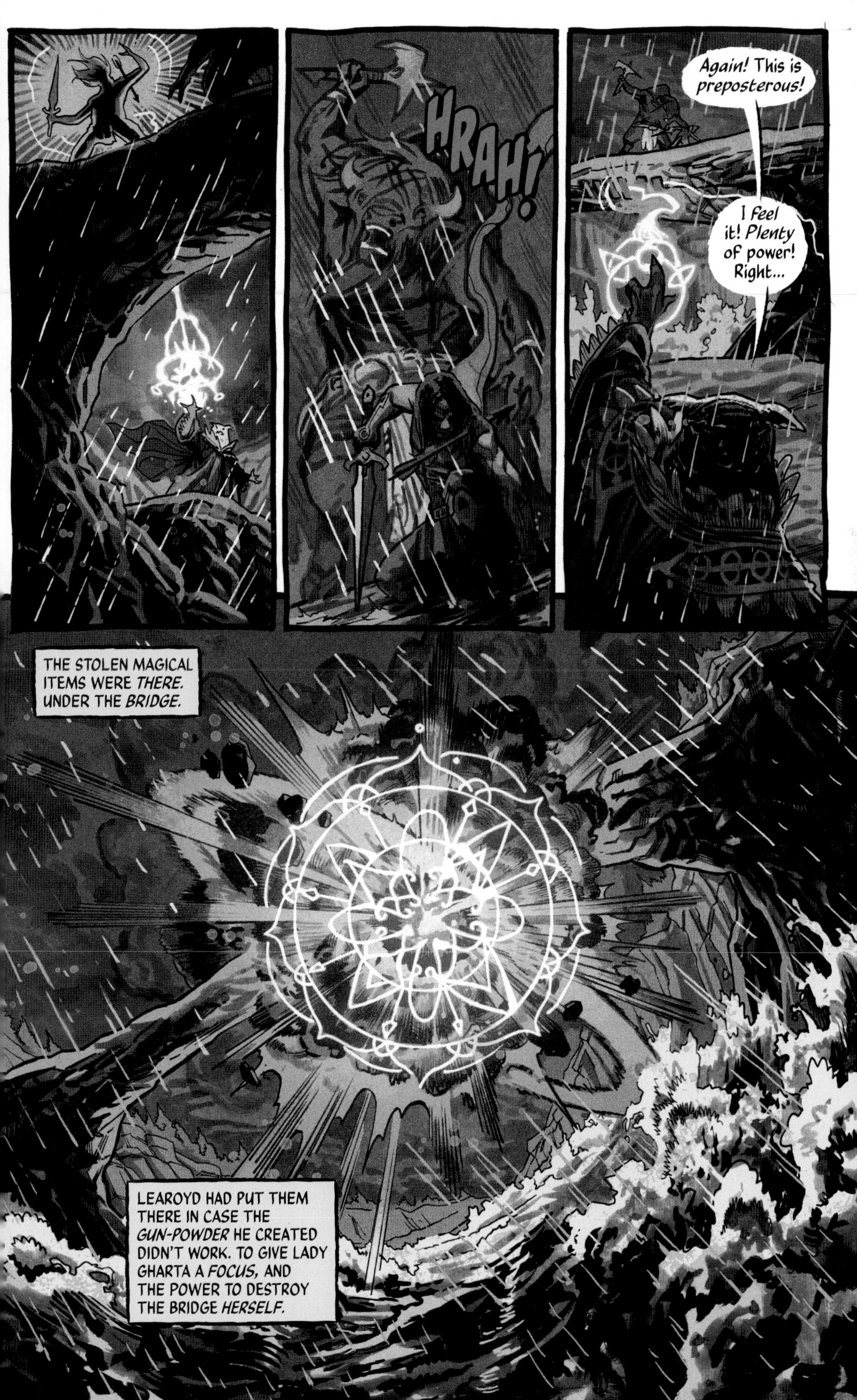
HRAH!
Again! This is preposterous!
I feel it! Plenty of power! Right...
THE STOLEN MAGICAL ITEMS WERE THERE. UNDER THE BRIDGE.
LEAROYD HAD PUT THEM THERE IN CASE THE GUN-POWDER HE CREATED DIDN'T WORK. TO GIVE LADY GHARTA A FOCUS, AND THE POWER TO DESTROY THE BRIDGE HERSELF.

BUT THIS –

Ha!
Hah!
Wh-
what – ?

IT WASN'T NECESSARY.
WE WERE SAVED. THE WIZARDS IN THE RESCUE HALL WOULD BE AT FULL POWER. THEY COULD HAVE CHASED OFF THE BISON EASILY.

IT WASN'T NECESSARY –

I did it! Praise the gods of defense and homeland security!
I'm the hero! I saved us all!

HE'D HAD A PLAN. BUT IT – IT –
I should have...I should have done as he said!
Maybe it... it would have been...

Easy, lad.
That pompous fool may think he's won, but –
No...

Eh?
Dusty!

SPLSH

DUSTY!
Sst!

No, child, no. Nothing you can do. Let it go, child.

Let it go...
Most glorious, Councillor!
All praise, sir! All praise!

You're our savior...